A Memory of Air House

MICHELLE JARVIS

PAPER MAGE PUBLISHING

So long as the memory of certain beloved friends lives in my heart, I shall say that life is good.

— HELEN KELLER

Contents

One

Ros sat in her father's cell for several hours while he related daring stories to her, most of which she knew were flat out lies. He couldn't grasp that they knew one another, couldn't remember a single event where she was present, and had instead assumed she was thinking of someone else. He'd immediately set out to remedy that by telling stories of his grand adventures.

Dimly Ros wondered if he always began new friendships by talking about himself so much. It wasn't something she'd noticed before. Then again, she'd spent her life hearing his stories told and retold, the details perfected after years of telling and rarely changing, so perhaps she hadn't realized this trait of his until now, when the stories weren't right. Maybe the embellishments were meant to impress his new companion, the only person he'd talked with in weeks. Or, perhaps, it was meant as a comfort to himself; after all, if he'd made it out of the situations he told her about, there was no reason to believe he couldn't make it out of this one.

She felt slightly guilty for tuning him out. It wasn't as if she'd done it intentionally; Ros was delighted to be with her father and see him alive, even if he didn't know who she was. But, try as she might to focus on the random stories he was telling, her mind wandered away from him while she tried to work out the details of what had happened and how she was going to make it right.

First, Graeme had trapped them. Now that her father's memory was gone, that didn't seem nearly as important as the rest of the story. Still, she needed to keep it at the front of her mind as a reminder that she couldn't afford to trust anyone until this whole mess was over. Maybe not even then. It was a liability she couldn't afford, especially after seeing how things had gone for her recently, and how everyone she trusted had been unworthy of her faith.

The second far more wonderful thing that was taking root in her head right now—though far less of a priority in comparison with needing to escape with her father—was that Cassian was alive. Gaius had been lying when he'd said otherwise. Despite everything that happened with the Great Match and her forced selection of Lyzandor Zolto, despite the awkward situation with Alaric, Cassian still loved her. He had returned for her, rescued her, stepped between her and danger and pushed her to safety...

Or had he?

The longer she thought about it, the more uncertain she became. She *wanted* him to love her; she *wanted* him to be her savior, but that didn't make it true. Cassian had been the one to send her away with Graeme. Did he do that to save her? Or was there a chance he knew Graeme was keeping her father hostage and this was all part of some nefarious plans to trap her along with the king? It would certainly be in line with what the other houses thought, but Ros had never bought into the idea that Cassian was evil just because he was from the Night house. Then again, everyone else had fooled her, so why not him? Could Cassian and the Night house be actively working against the throne?

She dwelled on these questions for far longer than she cared to admit. Ros wanted to have complete faith in Cassian and the strength of their relationship, but she couldn't. Not if she was being honest with herself. The longer she thought about it, the firmer her resolve became: she wouldn't believe that Cassian had anything to do with her captivity, or her father's. She couldn't. If she gave up on him, what did she have left?

Ironic, considering she had just told herself she couldn't trust anyone. It wasn't as if things between her and Cassian were going exceedingly well. He'd told her he loved her and seconds later, he'd said they could never be together. Not exactly the way she'd imagined things transpiring.

Ros shook her head, dislodging thoughts of Cassian. She wanted to make things right with him, but she couldn't allow him to rule her mind when there was so much else to deal with. Like the third and most dangerous thing on the mental list she was making: Datura Whimsy. The Moonchild had made a bargain with her, offering to grant her a wish. In an attempt to save the wish for when it was most dire, and a failure to consider the timing of the phases of the moon, Ros had missed her opportunity and lost the wish. Worse than that, Whimsy had taken her father's memories—or, at least, his memories of *her*. Now she was stuck in this cell with the man who had raised her, but who couldn't recall her in the least.

Footsteps clanged up the stairs. Ros and her father both turned toward the noise. A head popped up from the stairs, with wisps of white hair by his ears and a dark purplish nose, followed by the rest of the man's round body. He moved toward their cell, a tray rattling in his hands as he crossed the floor.

The man walked to the side of the room by the small door and was about to open it when he looked up and saw Ros. "What the devil are you doing in there, girl?"

Ros wasn't sure what to say. If he didn't recognize her, that was a good thing. She might be able to use it to her advantage. But *how* did he not recognize the first daughter of the kingdom?

"I was sent to check on the prisoner," Ros said. "The door was accidentally closed."

The man's bushy brows knit together. "And locked. From the outside."

"That can't be right. Someone must be playing a prank on me. Let me out and we'll clear everything up," she laughed.

"If I do that, and you're supposed to be in there, I'm a dead man."

"But if I'm telling you the truth and *he* finds me in here, discovering you left me, which of us will he blame?" Ros asked, batting her lashes.

The man's lips pressed together in a grim line. "Either way, I'm in trouble."

Ros looked around for anything to convince him her lie was the truth. Her eyes landed on the tray in his hands. "You've only been sent up with one meal. That alone should prove my words. If I were a prisoner, surely someone would send a second meal."

He considered this for a moment before saying, "I suppose that's true." He fiddled with the keys at his belt and said, "Come away from the prisoner and we'll get you out of there."

Ros put her hand on her father's shoulder and met his gaze. His expression was sad, as if she'd betrayed him. In a way, perhaps she had. She was leaving him behind, hoping she could figure out a way to get them both out of there. No matter how much she wanted to take him with her, it would do no good to get him free from the room, only to have him trapped in the Air house fortress.

"Hang on a little longer," she whispered. "I'll figure out a way to get you out of here."

King Tancred gave a small smile and Ros knew it was all he could muster. He didn't believe she would return for him, didn't believe he would get out of his prison, no matter how many daring escape stories he told. He especially didn't trust the girl he didn't know, who seemed to have just confirmed she was there by accident and in the employ of his captor. There was nothing she could say to change the way he saw her; Rosalinde's only way to prove herself was to set him free.

Ros stepped out of the door and the man slid the tray of food across the floor toward the sad king. The servant said, "Food's extra good today, Highness. Arina is in the kitchen this morning and she sent you an extra helping of pearsauce. I told her it's your favorite."

"Thank you, Henry. Your generosity abounds."

The exchange relieved Ros of some of her worry. Her father may be captive, but there was a modicum of kindness afforded to the kingdom's ruler, if not from his captor, then from those who served in silence.

Henry turned back to Ros and motioned her toward the exit, himself following behind. Just before they reached the stairs, her father called out, "Henry, wait. Do you have any news about my daughter?"

Rosalinde's breath caught in her chest. She turned her gaze to King Tancred, searching for anything that would let her know he remembered her, but his eyes were trained on Henry.

Henry sighed and shook his head. "Sorry, sire. Nothing new. The search party Queen Elsabet sent north is returning to Water house today after finding no trace of your presence. There is rumor of a skirmish of some sort, but the details are foggy and no one seems to know who was at the center of it. Handful of rebels, most likely."

"I see."

"There is one thing," Henry said, wincing, as if he didn't want to be the one to deliver the news. "Not related to your daughter, though."

"My wife?" Tancred asked.

Henry nodded. "Rumor has it she is betrothed."

Tancred's brows rose, but Ros already knew the words that awaited him. Still, she clenched her fist at her sides as Henry said, "To a Night house mage."

Henry started down the stairs. He didn't stay to see the look on the old king's face, but Ros saw it. It was a mix of confusion and hurt like she'd never seen. But as much as she wanted to rush back to him, to put her arms around him and promise things would be well, there was nothing she could do for him now.

She swallowed back the lump in her throat and followed Henry down the steps.

Two

They passed three more rooms with glass observation walls, but they were all empty. Ros was thankful for that; she wasn't sure how she was going to rescue her father and didn't need more prisoners weighing on her conscience. There was a noblewoman trapped in here as well—Florian's little sister, who Graeme claimed to be in love with—and rescuing her could prove as challenging, or more so, than freeing her father. Ros had no intention of simply leaving her there, but she also didn't have a plan, or even an inkling of an idea, for how to get her out.

That was a problem for future Ros. Right now, she had plenty of trouble without borrowing more from whatever was to come.

At the bottom of the stairs was a round room. There were no windows or doors that Ros could see, and the whole place was lit by candles. On the far wall was a row of hangers lined with cloaks and coats. Henry grabbed a massive coat and put it on. It was clearly made for a taller person, and when he pulled up the hood, it swallowed him head to heel, leaving only a glimpse of his icy blue eyes and bulbous nose.

"What are you waiting for, an invitation?" he asked. "Get your coat."

Ros surveyed those hanging on the wall and chose a plain brown cloak lined with rabbit fur. She didn't remember feeling cold when Graeme had brought her here, but then again, those first few minutes had blurred together as she realized his intent. Also, Henry's actions told her she couldn't trust her own memory when his insistence was showing her otherwise. At least with a cloak instead of a coat, she had the flexibility to move her arms if she needed to use her magic.

If she *could* use her magic. She still felt the heaviness pressing against her, the magic poisoning that kept her from being able to use the elements. It wasn't the painful, gasping thing that had hit her when she'd first set foot on the spire, but more like a steady weight resting against her chest.

For a moment, she wondered how long it took for Graeme and the other mages to grow accustomed to such a thing. She couldn't imagine living in a place that restricted magic in such a way, the toll it would take on someone to be constantly constricted by something out of their control. She almost felt sorry for the Elementalists of Air house. Almost.

The thought faded as soon as she pictured Graeme's face and the joy he'd shown when threatening to kill Rosalinde's sister, Elsabet. Ros felt her tender heart turn to steel in that moment. Air house would get none of her pity, and all her wrath.

"Are you well?" Henry asked.

Ros looked up, noting the furrowed brows peeking out from under his hood. "Yes, fine. I'm sorry. I must be more tired than I realized."

Henry glanced around, though Ros was certain no one else had entered the room. He said, "Be wary when saying such things. If the wrong person hears you, there will be hell to pay."

"For admitting my weariness?" Ros asked.

"Some see it as a slight against the house to say such things. To admit that your body is incapable of keeping up with the demands of our illustrious rulers is tantamount to treason."

"That makes little sense."

"Didn't anyone explain the rules before you began your service?" Henry asked.

Ros noted the way his eyes grew dark at his own question and she realized she'd made a mistake. She backtracked, saying, "Of course, but I thought it was an exaggeration. I was in such a hurry to serve Air house, I fear I let my naivety overpower my better judgment."

Henry grunted an affirmation, but Ros wasn't sure he believed her, and she needed him to if he was going to lead her out of here. She reached forward and put her hand on his forearm. "Please, I'm begging you, don't speak ill of me to the rulers. I know there's much for me to learn, and I will, with a little more time."

He seemed to soften and patted her hand. "Calm down, dear girl. Just keep quiet around the nobility and stay out of sight as much as possible. And always, no matter what, respond expediently when one of them asks something of you. Whether it is something in your line of work or not, acknowledge their request and make it happen, whatever it takes."

Ros nodded, despite the bile rising in her throat. Henry's instructions showed her exactly what it was like to live in Air house, to be subjected to the nobles' whims, and it made her sick. The worst part was when she realized there was probably a similar conversation happening with servants in the other houses all across Talabrih, even in her beloved Water house.

"Ready?" Henry asked, pulling Ros from her thoughts.

She nodded, though she was unsure what she was agreeing to. Henry stepped past her and pulled a lever on the wall. A gust of frigid air shot through the room, snowflakes whirling in and melting in the same breath. The reason she hadn't noticed a door was because there wasn't one—instead, there was an opening in the floor that led down a short ladder into the outside world.

Ros tried to erase the surprised expression from her features, but she knew her face always gave her away. She glanced toward Henry, thankful he was preparing to descend and hadn't looked her way. If she was going to pretend to be an Air house servant, she needed to get better at not looking like a gaping fool.

She crossed the room to follow Henry down the ladder. The metal was so cold it burned her fingers when she touched it. Still, it was nothing compared to the bitter cold assailing her. The wind tore at her as she descended, almost as if its whole creation and reason for existing was to attempt to rip Ros from safety and throw her to the ground far, far below. It continued to buffet her as she stepped down onto the platform below the spire. Though she pulled the cloak tight around herself and lifted the hood, the air was as sharp as icy daggers digging into every inch of exposed skin.

Attached to the platform was a swinging bridge. The ropes were white, with icicles hanging from them, and it was easy to see how Ros had missed them when she'd been looking down from atop the spire with Graeme. From above, they would've blended with the clouds. Now that she saw them, she couldn't *unsee* them. They crisscrossed the sky, connecting the sea-lavender colored spires like a giant spider's web.

Ros followed Henry onto the bridge. It swayed with each step, giving her a roiling feeling in her gut. It was much the same as when she'd first started using water magic all those years ago. She tried to remember her lessons from childhood about how to ride the waves; it had been so long ago, and she'd been such a terrible student, Ros couldn't recall much.

Her father's voice rang through her head in one

sudden, clear moment. He always told her to find a far-off spot and settle her mind on it. Ros wasn't sure she'd ever been able to do that as a child, but perhaps it wasn't too late to learn one of her father's lessons. She stared up to the closest spire, slick with rime, and used its solid presence to steady herself.

As she inched across the bridge, trying but unable to keep up with Henry's steady pace, she thought about what would happen if she fell. She probably wouldn't die—her magic would catch her, she hoped—but she wasn't sure how far out the magic poisoning extended from the spires or how long it took to get out of a person's system. So, even if she didn't die, there was a good chance she would still get severely hurt.

Ros didn't have time to deal with that, even if it was only in her mind. Instead of imagining herself flung to her doom, she gripped her hands tighter on the ropes on either side of her and pressed forward.

By the time she was halfway across, Henry had already reached the other side. Ros glimpsed him when she tore her eyes away from the glowing spire that now loomed in front of her. He was a comforting presence, for though she didn't really know him, she could see he was a kind man in his own way. He likely didn't choose to work for the people who imprisoned her father, it was just his unlucky lot in life. She couldn't fault him for that, even if he was a partici-pant in the king's captivity. As a servant to Air house, Henry was nearly as powerless as her father.

The next time she glanced at Henry, she was only a few

feet from the end of the bridge. He was stock-still, head bowed, standing in front of someone with a thick blue coat that looked as warm as a summer sky.

When the blue-coated man looked her way, Ros felt her heart drop to her feet. She stumbled her last step off the bridge, and for a moment, every imagined death flooded her mind once more. The man reached out to steady her and gave her a smile that lit his features, turning him into an oasis in the desert.

But Ros knew better. His kindness was a mirage, and Graeme Monsanato would not fool her again.

Three

Ros stood in front of the Air Elementalist, muscles taut, waiting for him to seize her, to yell, to show anger or disapproval. But he didn't. He kept smiling and staring down at her as if waiting for her to offer him... something. Ros wasn't sure what was happening.

"Forgive us, milord," Henry interceded, "for blocking your way. My companion is new in service to the greatest house in Talabrih, and she seems to be out of sorts."

Ros straightened her back and met Graeme's eyes, waiting for him to challenge Henry's words. A tiny crease formed at the inside of his left brow, but he shook his head and said, "Think nothing of it. The high path can be frightening to those who are encountering it for the first time."

"Yes, milord," Henry said, when Ros had failed to respond.

"What part of the Spires will you be serving, miss?"

His perfect smile stayed fixed on his face, and all at once Ros realized the fullness of Whimsy's curse. He hadn't simply pulled her from her father's memories; he erased any hint of her existence in this world. What was it the fae creature had said? She would be removed from the sight of all who knew her? It wasn't from their eyesight, it was from their minds. There would be no wrath toward her, no cruelty. There would be nothing but endless smiles, because Graeme had no idea who she was.

A laugh bubbled up, but she swallowed it back. It was a cruel trick Whimsy had played when they took away the memory of her, but in this moment, she was thankful for it. If no one remembered her, she had a better chance of escaping, of exacting revenge against those who had wronged her and the kingdom. She wasn't sure how, especially when this also likely meant that she wouldn't have any help making things right, but that was something she could figure out later.

From the corner of her eye, Ros saw Henry flapping his hands in a downward motion. It took her a second to realize what he was trying to convey, but as soon as she did, Ros dropped into a curtsy. She remembered the way her favorite chambermaid had behaved on her first day at Water house and tried her best to mimic her.

"Mercy, milord. I've never been so close to a great man such as yourself and I forgot my way. It won't happen again."

Graeme laughed as if she'd said the funniest thing he'd ever heard. "Rise, please. I am simply a servant of Air house, same as you. Now tell me, where have you been assigned?"

Ros scrambled for something that would explain why she was in the cell with her father. "Chamber pots, milord."

"You poor thing. That's the worst job."

"I'm happy to serve where I'm needed."

Though Ros had averted her gaze, she could feel Graeme's eyes roving over her. She forced herself to stand still, to allow him to weigh her worth however he saw fit, although every part of her wanted to recoil away from him. A servant would dare not cringe at his attention, so neither could she.

"What's your name?" Graeme asked.

"Ellenor," she said, recalling her maid once more. "Ellenor Thornby, milord."

"Today is your lucky day, Ellenor Thornby. I am in need of a new staff member for my rooms. Tell your mistress you have been reassigned and report to my chambers this afternoon for tea time."

Ros grit her teeth together to keep from growling out a curse. She dropped into another curtsy and, with unnatural sweetness, said, "Milord is too kind. How will I ever thank you?"

Graeme put his index finger under her chin and guided her gaze up to his. "Don't worry about that, darling. I'm sure I'll think of something."

He strode away, leaving Ros staring at his back as he crossed the swinging bridge. She felt as if she were welded to the platform below her. She couldn't move, couldn't breathe, couldn't shake away the disgust and anger churning inside her. How many young women had he coerced into his bed in exchange for an easier life?

Ros felt shame squirming in her gut. It wasn't because of what had just happened or the objective way Graeme had treated her; no, it was from never thinking about these situations before. She wanted to believe she understood her people's plight—had challenged Cassian when he said otherwise—but with each step further into their world, she seemed to understand less and less.

Or maybe this was the shock she needed to see them with open eyes. Being one of them would certainly educate her to the things she didn't see as a noblewoman, even if she was someone who tried to show kindness and under-standing to her people. There were some things she needed to learn on her own. Unfortunately, this was one of them.

She felt a presence beside her, and though Henry kept his hands in his coat's pockets, she felt his comfort as vibrantly as if he were wrapping his arms around her. "Are you all right?"

"No," she breathed.

But she would be. It was a vow pumping through her with every beat of her heart. She would stop those assholes from treating other people as if they were just toys in their playroom. There wasn't a plan yet for how she would do it, but Ros refused to let that behavior go unpunished.

"Come on," Henry said. "I'm freezing, and you need a drink."

HENRY GUIDED Ros through the maze of the Spires until at last they sat in front of a cooking fire. Ros had said little along the way, a numbness taking hold of her as the icy winds dampened her burning anger.

When they'd first arrived at the kitchen, Henry had leaned over and whispered something to the servant in charge. Ros didn't have to know what he said to understand the look of pity in the woman's eyes as she wrapped an arm over Rosalinde's shoulder and guided her to a stool.

A small girl approached with a hunk of bread drizzled in honey. She handed it to Ros, but before she could walk away, Ros grabbed her wrist. She stared up at the girl, noting the way she hunched her shoulders to make herself look smaller. The girl was older than Ros first thought; sixteen or seventeen, probably, though she made herself appear closer to twelve. Her hair was matted, but not in a way that indicated she hadn't combed it; rather, it looked strategic, as if she'd purposely disheveled herself. Below her left eye was a faded yellow bruise, nearly healed.

"It helps," the girl whispered. "A lot of them won't touch a servant if they aren't clean."

Ros tapped under her own eye and said, "But some still do."

The girl pulled her arm out of Rosalinde's grasp and walked away.

ROS EXPECTED GRAEME'S "TEA TIME" to be later in the afternoon, as it was in Water house. Instead, he preferred it in lieu of a midday meal. When the hour grew close, the old woman guided Ros in the practice of everything she would need to do to serve *Master* Graeme. He took both sugar and milk with his tea. If it was only warm instead of hot when the servant arrived, he would punish them. No one would tell her exactly what that meant.

A page arrived shortly before service to advise the kitchen that Graeme had a guest. In addition to another cup for his companion, Graeme wanted her to bring bread, butter, honey, fruit, cheese, and a variety of dried meats. By the time everything was gathered, it was too much for Ros to carry, and she was given a small pushcart. It was also ten minutes past Graeme's tea time, and Ros didn't miss the staff exchanging nervous glances.

She said goodbye to Henry and the head of the kitchen, cursing herself for not getting the woman's name. She tried to remember all the names of the Water house staff, and it chafed her that she hadn't made the same effort here, even if she didn't plan to be here long.

The young page who'd brought word of Graeme's guest led her back to the nobleman's sitting room. She felt as if she needed a moment to compose herself, but before she'd even reached the door, the page opened it and ushered her in. So, Ros plastered a smile on her face as she prepared to meet Graeme and whatever unpleasant person would be there as his guest.

When Ros entered the room, her heart nearly jumped out of its chest. At the table across from Graeme was a mage with olive skin and eyes so dark they seemed as if they absorbed all the light from the room. He looked up at her, his smile faltering just a fraction before he turned his attention back to Graeme.

It was enough. That tiny twitch at the corner of his lips sent Rosalinde's heart flying. Not only was Cassian Scalise here, but he recognized her.

Four

"I still don't get why you're here," Graeme said.

Ros looked up, thinking he was addressing her, but his eyes were focused on Cassian.

"I wanted to check on you after everything that happened at Earth house."

"Honestly, Cas, I can barely remember even being there. It was of so little consequence, I've wiped it from my mind."

"You don't remember fighting for the queen?"

"Of course that's what we were doing there," Graeme said, waving Ros away as she offered him some bread. "We live to serve Queen Elsabet. But by the time I arrived, there was nothing left to do. The uprising had been addressed, so I returned home posthaste."

"Alone?" Cassian asked. He glanced at Ros, and though she tried to shake her head to dismiss his attention, it was too late.

"You sly devil," Graeme said with a chuckle. "Yes, I was alone that night, but I don't plan to be tonight."

He reached over and ran a hand down Rosalinde's leg. She flinched at the touch, then ducked her head in an attempt to seem demure instead of disgusted. Slipping around the table, Ros set out the last of the food. She put a cup and saucer on Cassian's plate and noticed his hands gripping the table's edge so tightly his knuckles were white.

"Is milord well?" Ros asked, her voice barely a whisper.

Graeme pounded a fist on the table and growled, "I showed you kindness for your indiscretion this morning, Ellenor, but speaking to my guests is far beyond appropriate."

"No, please," Cassian said, waving a hand at Graeme while he moved the other to his temple. "She's perceptive, it seems. I'm feeling quite ill."

"So sudden," Graeme said, brows furrowing.

Cassian nodded. "Is there somewhere I could rest for a little while? I fear recent events have taken more from me than I initially realized."

"Of course, friend. I'll have a room prepared," Graeme said. He stood and walked to the door. Turning back, he asked, "How long will you be staying?"

"I'll be out of your hair before dinner," Cassian said. "I'm sure it's nothing but fatigue."

Graeme nodded and strode out into the hall. As soon as he was gone, Cassian bolted up from his chair and wrapped his arms around Rosalinde, pulling her against his chest. It was a brief embrace, only enough to seemingly prove to him she was really there, before he released her and asked, "What the hell is going on?"

"He doesn't know who I am."

"Head injury?" Cassian asked, his lips turning up in a smile as if the idea pleased him.

"No one does," she said, rushing out the words. "A fae wiped all memories of me."

"Not all. I remember you."

"And you shouldn't. It doesn't make sense."

"There's nothing in all the worlds that could make me forget you, Ros. Even when I try. Gods help me, I *have* tried."

In that moment, Ros felt like she could fly. If Cassian never said another word to her, that would be enough to keep her heart beating. She said, "It's you and me. It's always going to be the two of us, no matter what. Don't fight it anymore."

He pressed his forehead against hers and said, "We have to get out of here. Now."

"I can't," she said. "He has my father."

He pulled back from her. "Here? You've seen him?"

"He's in one of the spires. Florian's sister is there, too. Magic doesn't work there."

Cassian cursed and pulled away from her, pacing. "This is fine; we can do this." He mumbled to himself for a few seconds, saying, "Magic doesn't work while you're within range of what? The spires? But Graeme can still use the elements?"

"I don't know how, and there's no time to sort it out. He'll be back any second," she hissed.

Cassian spun toward her. "I'll go to a room and rest for a while. When I can slip away, I'll get to your father."

"It's too dangerous," she said.

"Let me worry about that. In the meantime, you need to find somewhere to hide."

"What? No. I won't hide while you handle the danger."

"Please don't argue. It will be easier for me to focus on everything else if I know you're safe. Get out of sight while you can. I'll find you during the nobles' dinner. There's no telling what he'll do if..."

Cassian trailed off. Graeme stood in the doorway, a strange look on his face. "Am I interrupting something?"

"Just me trying to corrupt your maid," Cassian said, forcing a smile. "Guess I'm not too sick for *some* things."

The two men laughed while Ros tried to remember that Cassian was saying those things to protect her. It didn't work. The bile that had been rising in her throat all morning chose that moment to come out, and Ros turned her head and puked on the rug.

Graeme made a disgusted sound and barked, "Clean that up!"

"She may have caught whatever has me feeling ill."

"Have you been *that* close to her?" he asked, brows raising.

"Not nearly as close as I would like, but alas, her attention wouldn't stay with me."

Graeme smirked. "Of course not. She knows who her master is."

Ros didn't look at either of them, afraid of what they would see on her face if she acknowledged their words. She knew Cassian was only saying what he had to—or at least that was what she wanted to believe—but it still infuriated her. What if this was how all the noblemen spoke of their maids? What if Cassian had said these things before, and this version of him was more accurate than she wanted to think?

The rage burning through her heated her cheeks, made her nearly bare her teeth in anger and frustration, and it would give her away in an instant if Graeme noticed. These were not the reactions of a maid.

"Perhaps another servant could clean while you send her to rest," Cassian said.

"Fine," Graeme replied. Turning to Ros, he said, "You're excused. Send another to clean up. Take care of yourself today, as I'll expect to see you back here tomorrow morning for my bath where we can get properly acquainted."

Ros nodded, whispered her thanks, and rushed out of the room. Her disgust toward Graeme had given her an excuse to go missing for the rest of the day. Now she just had to stay out of the way until she and Cassian could rescue her father and she was in the clear. With Rosalinde's natural predilection for trouble added to her desire to help, it was basically impossible for things to go well.

Ros moved through the halls on silent feet. She did not know where she was going, but everywhere she walked, it was done so with a fast pace and her head down. To her surprise, no one stopped her. Then she realized that to the others, she was just another servant completing another task for another noble. Stopping her could mean adding to their own trouble, and none were willing to do that.

She tried to keep a mental note of everywhere she went, but it was difficult to keep up. The spires were all shaped the same and the floors each had a similar layout. It wasn't like the spire with the cells, where each floor was dedicated to one room. No, the larger spires had dozens of rooms for a variety of purposes. After crossing the swinging bridge into the fourth one, she gave up trying to figure them out.

The more distance she put between herself and Graeme, the better she felt. She was also putting space between her and Cassian, but not for long. She was determined to meet him later, to take hold of him and not let go this time. Everyone else in the world had forgotten her, except Cassian; that had to mean something.

It took Ros a few minutes to notice how quiet this spire was. The ever-present stream of servants and guards trickled off as she climbed higher, until eventually she was the only person walking the floors. It seemed like the perfect place to hide for a few hours without fear of being found.

On the fifth floor, Ros found a library. It wasn't as big as the one at Water house, but perhaps she would find some texts here that she didn't have at home. Plus, it would keep her occupied while she waited for the afternoon to pass.

Ros walked the perimeter of the room first, looking for an attendant that wasn't there, and scouting a secluded spot to sit and read. There were a couple of spots in the room that seemed made for hiding. Ros chose the one that left her facing the door so she could see anyone who came in, though they wouldn't be able to see her.

"What should I read?" she murmured.

Look for something about the Cradles.

Ros jerked her head up from the shelf she was browsing and spun around. She was alone. "Who's there?"

Just me. In your head. Have you forgotten so quickly?

She swallowed. She had, in fact, forgotten the voice that she'd heard after absorbing the Night Cradle. He'd been silent since she'd left Earth house, and with everything else going on, it was easy not to think about him.

Ros wasn't sure what she was supposed to think about him, anyway. She had no idea where he came from, only that it wasn't from the magic itself, and that he seemed to have thoughts independent from her own. She said, "I don't have to listen to you."

Oh really? You were awfully accepting of my advice before.

"You're part of my imagination."

We both know that isn't true.

"Fine, then. What are you?"

I think you mean who *am I? Either way, the question is irrelevant.*

"Irrelevant?" she hissed.

The voice shushed her. *Quiet down, unless you want to get caught.*

"You know I don't," Ros whispered.

Then let me help you. Two minds are better than one, after all.

She bit her lip, unsure. The voice *had* helped her before, but that didn't mean it didn't have ulterior motives. "Tell me why I should listen to you."

Because you don't want to die.

"No one does."

You don't want your family and friends to die.

"Of course not."

They will, if you don't get out of this mess.

"I guess you have a plan?"

I do. The first step is getting some information. Hold your hand out toward the books.

She lifted her hand, then changed her mind and pulled it back. "I will agree to your help, but I don't trust you."

Fair enough.

"And I want to know your name."

You don't need—

"Nevertheless," she interrupted. "I want to know who I'm talking to."

There was a long pause, and she thought he might go silent again, but finally, he said, *Lucasian.*

"That wasn't so hard," she said.

After a pause, he said, *Your hand?*

Ros held out her hand. There was a faint red glow around her fingers. She couldn't do magic because of the strange poisoning in Air house, but that didn't seem to affect Lucasian. Whether that was good or bad, Ros wasn't sure.

As she walked down the rows of books, the color around her fingers changed. It shifted to orange, then yellow, and lastly to green.

Stop, Lucasian said. *There's something here that can help us.*

Ros paused, her fingers dancing over the spines. A shock bit her finger as an electric current struck out from one of the books. "This one, then."

And the one with the dark green cover on the third shelf. Grab that brown one, too. The one with the dark stain on it.

"Blood," she whispered.

Probably.

Lucasian didn't elaborate, and Ros didn't press. She wasn't sure what kind of magic he had or what it told him about the books, and she was glad she didn't have to know, especially if someone's blood was dried into the book pressed against her chest.

She secreted away into the corner of the room with the three books and the stranger's voice inside her head. She wasn't sure exactly what she was looking for, but she opened the book anyway, saying, "We've got five hours until dinner, and that's when Cassian will make his move."

Well then, Lucasian said, *it's time to get to work. I hope you're a fast reader.*

Five

Ros flipped through the pages of the book that had shocked her, searching for information about the Cradles. She found a mention here and there in the book, but nothing more than what she already knew. She was about to put the book away when she found a passage about the fae.

You can move to the next book, Lucasian said.

"I can, but I'm not done with this one."

There's nothing of value in this one.

"Maybe not to you and whatever your endgame is, but I have other business besides the Cradles."

We don't have time for this.

Ros noticed an edge to his voice. There was something here that he didn't want her to see. "It will take only a moment if you'll be quiet."

There was a slight grumble inside her head, but he said nothing else. She had grumbles of her own building up, though she dare not think them right now. Still, she knew eventually she would have to figure out who this voice belonged to and why he was in her head. Right now just wasn't the time.

Ros read the few paragraphs about the fae, then read it again. It didn't quite make sense to her. There were a few words she didn't understand and without them, the entire section lost its context.

"Do you know this phrase?" she asked, resting her finger under *Tuath Dé*.

Yes.

She sighed. It seemed he would not make this easy for her. "Will you tell me what it means?"

Ask nicely.

"Please?"

He sighed, or what seemed to qualify for a sigh in thought form. *It doesn't have a perfect translation into your language. Roughly, it means* tribe of the gods. *Or, more accurately, a collection of gods.*

"And this one? Please?"

Sahlegh? He asked. *It means to* rend.

"So, if I'm reading this correctly, the fae and humans lived together until the gods split their worlds." When he didn't respond, Ros went on: "But why would they do that? And if the worlds are split, how can the fae still come through to this side?"

Why do you care about the fae when we are in need of a way to save this *world?*

"I'd like my father to know who I am," she said. "The

only way to do that is to get back what was taken from me, if that's even possible. What's the point of living in this world if I've lost everyone I love?"

You can get your father back, Lucasian said.

His words were so simple, so matter-of-fact, Ros almost laughed. "Easier said than done."

It's easily done, if you know what you're doing. Luckily for you, I do.

"You can restore his memories?"

I can help you capture and command the one who stole them, force them to return what was taken.

"How?"

Everything depends on the Cradles. They are the weakest spot between the worlds. If you go to one and speak the right incantation, you can call specific fae through the worlds and force them to answer to you.

"How do you know how to do that?"

I know how to do many things. I could explain it to you, though you've already said you do not trust me, and rightly so. There is no way to guarantee my words are true, or that what I might teach you is meant for your human mind.

"Meant for me or not, I still need to know it."

As you wish, he said. *I will do this for you, and in exchange, I will ask for your help.*

"What do you need me to do?"

I'll tell you when the time is right.

She'd already been burned once by the fae creature, and now she was dealing with something she knew even less about. "I will not agree to help you without knowing the cost."

I will not harm you or those you love, Lucasian said. *I will take nothing from you but time.*

"Time can be a heavy price."

Ten days, my dear. No more, no less.

It sounded too good to be true. And too much like Whimsy's deal for her comfort. "You still haven't told me what I'd be doing."

I cannot see the future. I only know that for now, I need you to be my body, since mine is... elsewhere. You will transport me home, and help me return to my former life, if possible.

"Fine," she said, the word slipping from her lips before she had time to think about it. But since she was already carrying him around, it didn't seem like much change was necessary.

Excellent. Now that we've reached an agreement, put down that nonsense book and pick up the bloody brown one.

"You're a bossy one," she murmured.

You have no idea.

HOURS PASSED IN RELATIVE SOLITUDE. Twice she saw someone come into the library, but neither of them bothered her. In fact, neither seemed to notice she was there at all. She was grateful for their oversight, but something about it felt off. Though she tried to keep her focus on the books, something wriggled at the back of her mind, a tiny warning she couldn't name.

When the afternoon passed into evening, Ros roused herself and put away the books. Lucasian seemed content with what he'd learned, though much of it made little to no sense to her and he was in no mood to discuss it. He might be pleased with the knowledge they'd gathered, but his attitude had soured as the minutes ticked by, leaving him a silent passenger in her head.

Ros slipped through the quiet halls of the library spire and out onto the ice bridge. In the distance, the sun drifted ever closer to the dark mountaintops, soon to sink below the sharpened talons jutting into the evening sky. She vaguely wondered if the bridges were more treacherous at night, and if Air house had a history of losing servants to slippery falls.

She looked around at the collection of spires closest to her. They were all roughly the same size and shape, made of the same material, and nearly identical in color. Ros wasn't sure how anyone kept them straight. But she needed to figure it out, fast. Cassian was somewhere nearby—her father as well—and she intended to leave with both of them.

The sound of shouting drew her attention. Several spires to her right, she watched as a squad of guards wrestled someone out onto the bridge. Ros couldn't see the person clearly thanks to the last of the sunlight leaving them in silhouette, but whoever it was, they were not going without a fight.

Faster than Rosalinde's eyes could track, they whirled around and sent two guards flying off the bridge. A moment later, the guards were flung back up onto the platform under the spire. She remembered how the same thing had happened to her when she'd tried to jump from the top of the tower. There was some sort of barricade that prevented people from falling, and had probably saved plenty of lives through the years. Magic protected this floating city, both the nobles and the commoners, but the power on display was only known to the privileged few.

Follow them, Lucasian said.

"Are you crazy?" she whispered. "That's the surest way to get caught."

They'll lead us to your father.

"There could be another place they keep prisoners."

There most certainly is, he said. *But this one is going to the noble holdings.*

"You don't know that."

At some point, your distrust will grow tiresome. He sighed, then continued, *I have no proof, if that is what you want. But I* know *it is the right move.*

There was no reason for her to listen, but no reason not to, either. It would do him no good to lie to her; if she got caught, so did he. If he was right, perhaps she could help her father escape and speed up the process of getting out of there.

Ros jogged the length of the bridge she was on, more confident now that she knew she wouldn't fall to her death if she slipped. At the base that connected to the spire, she spun around until she saw the guards again and oriented herself toward them. Every spire wasn't connected, so she needed to figure out which bridge to take at this junction so she could get to the one with the guards.

Her instincts told her to take the next right, but as she traced the trajectory with her eyes, she realized one would end up taking her below the spire she was aiming for. So, against her gut, she took the one on the left.

This one seemed to lead away from her goal, initially anyway. She could see the way it circled around to the right place; she just had to take the long way. That wasn't a problem for her though, because as she moved around the spires, she could see the guards enter the spire with their prisoner and, a few minutes later, leave without them.

She made it to the bridge the guards had fallen off and scurried across. At the base of the spire was a ladder. It wasn't like the doors and stairwells that led into the other spires; no, this was definitely the ladder she'd climbed down earlier when Henry led her away from her father's prison.

"You were right," she said as she climbed.

I'm quite good at being right.

Ros smirked, but neither commented further. His ego seemed big enough as it was, and she had no desire to inflate it further. Secretly, she was thankful he was there, even if she didn't know who or what he was. He seemed able to see the big picture when she was too focused on the details, and it had already saved her more than once.

There was no one in the round room when she reached it. She climbed the next two flights, surprised each time when they were empty. Mouth dry and fists clenched at her side, Ros stepped onto the fourth floor.

There was a new prisoner in the observation room on this floor. It wasn't unexpected. The guards had left without him, so he had to be somewhere in the spire. When the man turned to face her and she saw Cassian's handsome face, that didn't astound her either. Part of her had known it would be him, even if she hadn't been able to say it aloud.

It was the tears in his eyes that were the truly astonishing things. She'd never seen him be anything but strong. Now, he seemed broken. The man she'd left in the tea room that afternoon was not the same one standing in the glass cell before her.

He looked at her, lips trembling, and said, "Run."

Six

Ros stepped toward the glass, but Cassian shook his head. "Go, now."

"I'm not leaving without you," she said.

"You have to."

"There's nothing you can say to change my mind."

"He knows, Ros. Graeme knows you're not a maid. He'll be searching for you next."

"How?" she breathed.

"They caught me snooping around and took me for questioning."

He wouldn't tell them about you, so what is he hiding?

"There's something you're not saying," she said.

His dark eyes met hers. He swallowed hard, and it was clear he didn't want to tell her whatever was going on. Finally, he said, "Graeme has a Mind mage."

Ros flinched at the words. There were old stories about such powers, dark tales that were used to frighten young children, but there hadn't been an actual Mind mage in Talabrih in centuries. Then again, she'd thought the same about Night mages until Cassian showed up.

Night mages had been a strange revelation for her, but Mind mages were something else entirely. Myths about them claimed they could infiltrate your thoughts and poke around inside your mind, revealing things so far buried in the victim's subconscious, even they might not realize what was there.

The scary part, though, was what they could do once they were inside a mind. Or at least, what the rumors and old stories *said* they could do. She'd never believed they were even real, but the tales said they could see someone's thoughts and memories, and they could use the mind to haunt that person in a dozen different ways. Or worse, they could destroy the person with just a thought.

The words stuck in Rosalinde's throat and she didn't want to ask, but she had to: "What did they do to you?"

Cassian shook his head. "It wasn't as bad as you're thinking. They weren't trying to hurt me. They could have, but they didn't."

"They still need you."

And now they need you, Lucasian thought. *They probably couldn't sort through it all from his memories, because no one else remembers you. But they know you're part of* something, *even if they don't know what. You're compromised.*

"Forget all that," Ros murmured. Cassian furrowed his brows, but didn't say anything as Ros continued. "Our goal is still the same. We have to get you and my father out of here."

"You have to get out, Ros. There's not enough time for a rescue."

"I can't leave you."

"You have to. Get to safety. Figure out a way to get help. We'll still be here when you do."

Silence stretched between them until Lucasian finally said, *He's right.*

Ros whispered, "Isn't there anything you can do?"

Lucasian and Cassian both said, "No."

"I found out a couple of things that can help you," Cassian said. "First, the reason Graeme's magic works is that he has an amulet that prevents the magic poisoning from seeping into him. Only the highest nobility have them, while everyone else suffers under it. Even the servants without magic say it affects them, though not as forcefully as an Elementalist."

"If I could get the amulet—"

"You can't. Maybe before, when he was trying to get under your dress, but not now. He has guards on call, and you don't have the power or authority to do anything about it."

I might be able to take care of that for you once I am restored.

Lucasian's magic was the only kind working in this place, unaffected by the Air house wards, and he wasn't operating at full power. She stored the thought away to chew on later.

"So, I sneak in and steal it from him while he's asleep."

"No. You leave and come back with your sister's throne backing you. Even then, there's a chance Air house will put up a fight, and this place is a fortress that won't be easily beaten."

How do you get out of this godsforsaken place?

"I can't leave, even if I was willing to abandon you," Ros said. "You saw what happened to the guards when you tried to throw them over."

Cassian smiled. "Something about surviving that made them far too free with information."

"What are you saying?"

"I knew they'd fly back up. It's one of the greatest spells in Air house's history, and one they're quite proud of even if they don't fully understand how it works. Knowing it's there gives them security, but it also gives them loose lips. They were so giddy to be returned to safety that they made a joke about being glad they weren't near the spell's gap."

"Gap?"

"I knew there had to be one, because how else could the lower nobility come and go? There has to be somewhere to get in and out of the place without being shot back up by magic."

"And?"

"There's a landing site outside the boundaries of the spell. It's connected by a bridge, like all the other spires. You just have to figure out which one it is."

"I can find it and come back for you."

"Or you can save yourself, like I need you to."

"If I run from this place, if I abandon you—"

"There's no other way."

"I don't want to be separated from you again."

Cassian held up his hands and plastered on a ridiculous smile. "You know where to find me. I promise I'll wait here for you."

"What if—"

"No," he said. "There's no point dwelling on things that aren't real. You are going. Not because you want to, but because all our hope now rests on you getting out of here. I trust you to do this, to get to safety and come back when you have more than just hope. Don't let me down."

Seven

Ros crouched at the base of the landing tower. It had taken her nearly an hour to figure out which one it was, and another forty minutes to make her way across the bridge. Maybe she could've gotten here faster, crossed the bridge sooner, scurried up the spire quicker... but she didn't want to.

Saying goodbye to Cassian had been a struggle. He kept urging her to leave, and he told her she wasn't abandoning him, but damn it, that's what it felt like. She didn't have time to say farewell to her father. Even if she'd gone to his cell, he would only know her as the girl who worked for his captor. She didn't want to see the disappointment in his eyes again; honestly, she wasn't sure she could survive it.

Lucasian had remained quiet since they'd left the prison. He'd spoken up once to make sure she took the correct path once they'd figured out which spire was the right one, but nothing since.

She wasn't sure why his silence bothered her. Maybe it was because he'd been all too eager to lend his voice to support Cassian when they talked of her leaving. Or perhaps it was the nagging thought that he'd gotten what he wanted so now he could sit back and enjoy the ride. But mostly, it was just Ros wishing she had someone to comfort her while her feelings were flooding through her, even if that someone was just a voice in her head.

You can't hide here forever.

Not for the first time, she wondered if he could read her thoughts. She was too afraid to ask and find out for sure.

"Another guard could come by here any minute," she said. "I don't want them to see me climbing into the spire."

Guards had been swarming the bridges for the last hour, and several had passed her while she had been hiding, getting a little too close for comfort. But they both knew that wasn't the reason she was stalling.

You'll see him again.

"You said you can't see the future."

I don't have to see the future to know you'll figure out a way through this. There's a ferocity to your love that says you'll do whatever it takes for the people you care about.

"I will," she said, her voice cracking.

All you have to do for them right now is climb up into the spire.

Into the chilly night air, she whispered, "I'm scared."

Me, too. But you're not alone. I'm here. The hearts of those men are here, counting on you to save them. So, don't think about what you're afraid of; think about why you can't let fear win.

Ros climbed. This spire was shorter than the others—only two stories—but it was also at a higher elevation than even the tallest of the other structures. As she reached the top and stepped out onto the landing pad, she could see the whole of Air house spread out before her.

There were a dozen spires with yellow light streaming from windows she hadn't been able to see from below. The whole place was laid out in a diamond shape, though she hadn't realized it while she was in it. Seeing it from above gave her a much better idea of how to navigate it for next time.

There would most definitely be a next time.

There were shouts below. Ros looked down to see a handful of guards pointing up at her. Her heart hammered in her chest, but she knew they were too late. They wouldn't make it to her in time, when all she had to do was jump.

Ros stepped to the edge of the platform facing away from Air house. From this side, there was only the velvety black of night. She knew there were mountains below, rivers and trees and rocks, but she couldn't see any of that.

She closed her eyes and took a deep breath. Without giving herself another moment to talk herself out of it, Ros jumped.

THE AIR BUFFETED her as she fell, tumbling end over end like a rock thrown from a great height. It had only been seconds, but she felt like she'd been falling forever, like she would always be falling. Some little part of her reveled in it.

Open your eyes.

Instead, she squeezed them shut tighter. If she opened them, things became real again. She didn't want *real*.

Who will save them if you're dead?

As much as she hated him for it, Lucasian was right. Ros opened her eyes. She was closer to the ground than she thought. She called to her magic.

Nothing happened.

Again, she reached for the water element that had been her constant companion since she was a child. It was silent.

Panic overtook her as she closed the gap between her and certain death. She only had seconds.

The Cradle. Think of the Cradle!

Ros remembered the darkened circle. The way it had been hidden by an illusion the first time she set foot there. Cassian and his mother, Ombretta, had fought the darkness there. When she'd returned to the Night Cradle, she'd captured it, absorbing the power within herself. When she'd left, the burned circle was in full bloom.

Ros hit the ground hard, her breath knocked from her body in a painful rush. She looked out over a blooming circle where once there had been nothing but dark and rot. Her body was sore, but the fall had not been as bad as it could've been without the dormant magic throwing her to the Cradle instead of against the rocky terrain under Air house. She still hadn't regained the breath that was forced out of her by the impact, and she laid there a moment, gasping for another. There would definitely be a bruise on her chest later.

Still, she was alive. For now, that was enough.

After a few minutes, her breathing was back to normal, and she pushed herself up to look at the circle of wildflowers ringed by trees. The full realization of what had happened was just now becoming clear to her. It hadn't been her Tsunami power that saved her—it had been the Night.

Well, wasn't that fun?

Ros wanted to be a smartass right back to him, but she couldn't muster the indignation. Instead, she laughed. And laughed. After a few seconds, she realized Lucasian was laughing, too.

"I don't think I'd recommend it to anyone that has another choice," she said after their laughter subsided.

If I had a body, I probably would've pissed myself.

"I'm honestly surprised I didn't."

You were too busy screaming.

"Was I?"

I'm not surprised you didn't notice since there were a bunch of yelling guards, a monstrous blast of wind, and the ground all trying to violently kill us.

"But it didn't," Ros said. "We live to fight another day."

And fight we shall. But first, we have work to do. You've got a fae to call forth and subdue.

In the excitement of all that had happened, Ros had forgotten about her arrangement with Lucasian. He would help her call Whimsy to her and she would return her father's memories. The time she would owe him later in exchange for his help seemed of little consequence now when faced with the prospect of getting back all that had been lost.

"What do I do?"

It's simple. I'll tell you a spell that will call them to this world. When I do, you'll bind their will to yours so that they must do your bidding.

"That sounds easy enough."

It is, once you know what you're doing.

"And you're sure you do?"

I guarantee it. The hard part will be that you'll need to trust me.

"What if I can't?"

Then jumping from that tower was pointless.

"You're sure there's no other way?"

If there is, I don't know it.

She sighed. Lucasian had helped her repeatedly. Sure, maybe a large part of that was self-preservation, but Ros wanted to believe at least part of it was coming from an individual who cared about more than themself. She barely knew him, but like it or not, she needed to trust him.

"Fine," she said. "I can do this. *We* can do this. Together."

That's very bold of you.

"My future is in your hands, just like it has been since the Cradle. You saved me back there, and I couldn't have done it without you," she said matter-of-factly.

Well then, he said, the hint of a smile in his voice. *I'm glad you can recognize this partnership for what it is. I save the day, and you frolic your way back to my body.*

"I don't frolic."

Not yet, but we can work on it.

Ros sighed, but did so with a smile. Lucasian was certainly unlike anyone she'd met before, but right now, that was exactly what she needed. If she was truly going to make this work, it would be with his help. She took a deep breath and said, "Tell me what to do."

Eight

With the summoning complete, Rosalinde dropped her hands and waited. She feared it might take a while for anything meaningful to happen, but it was only a moment before the proof of the spell's effectiveness was before her eyes.

Datura Whimsy stood in a patch of silver that lit the Night Cradle. They had the form of the sweet little creature she'd first met, made of moonlight and wisps of silver, barely rising to Rosalinde's hip. But after her last encounter with the Moonchild, Ros knew this appearance was only a half truth. There was another version of Whimsy when the moon was out of view, and it was beastly and terrible to behold.

"Isn't this a surprise," Whimsy said, their sing-song voice like a bell tinkling through the air.

"It shouldn't be," Ros said. "You had to know I'd find you eventually, considering what you took from me."

Whimsy smiled, their sharp teeth glittering like dagger points as they reflected the moonlight. "I gave you a fresh start, Rosalinde Adara Managold. You should thank me."

"You removed my existence from the minds of those I love."

"And those you don't," Whimsy said. "Not to mention those who despise you, the enemies who wish you harm. Now is your chance to escape the dangers of your past and forge a new future, free of the pain and fears that have followed you through your young life. You are a stranger to all, equally."

"Is that supposed to make me feel better?"

Whimsy shrugged. "Your feelings are none of my concern."

Rosalinde's blood boiled. This creature had taken everything from her. How could they be so callous about it, as if what they'd done meant nothing? She gritted her teeth and focused on the words Lucasian had made her memorize from the book in the library. Ros would make the fae creature pay for what they'd done. Whimsy might not care about her feelings right now, but they would in a few minutes when Ros had control of them.

She spoke the words from the book in the fae language she didn't understand, repeating them back exactly as Lucasian had instructed. The words left a strange taste in her mouth, bitter and clinging to her tongue. She followed the fae words with the translation Lucasian had given her: "From dust to bone, blood to heart, the strings that bind will never part." A double binding, according to the voice in her head, though he seemed to think once was enough. Ros wasn't willing to risk losing the Moonchild again by saying something wrong, so this had seemed like a good idea when they were making plans As she spoke the binding aloud, there was a heaviness in them she hadn't felt when they'd been on paper.

A cloud of dust rose around the Moonchild's ankles, but the fae still smirked at Ros, seeming wholly unconcerned. "Handy trick, but useless in the hands of a mortal."

She continued, "From sky to ground, sun to rain, the bond that seals, life will drain."

Ros watched Whimsy's brows furrow and they strained against the words, but she could see that it still wasn't enough.

Now, you have to finish binding them in the language of the Tuath Dé.

I don't know how, Ros thought.

She felt Lucasian's annoyance roil through her. Annoyance? *What nerve.* This voice had been hitching a ride with her since she'd taken the power of the Night Cradle, and he had the audacity to be annoyed that she couldn't speak a language she'd never heard? Ros wanted to show him exactly how annoyed *she* was right back at him, but she couldn't risk pissing off the only help she had.

Here's where the trust comes in. Repeat after me and I'll get you through this.

Ros listened as Lucasian's words lilted in a language so painfully beautiful to listen to that she found a tear rolling down her cheek unbidden.

It's beautiful, she thought.

Repeat it, Lucasian commanded. *Quickly, before you lose your chance.*

Lucasian spoke the words again inside her head, and though she was certain her voice didn't have the silky quality that his did, nor could she speak with the same fluidity when she spoke the words, the effect was the same.

Whimsy's eyes filled with tears, and they fell to their knees. The dust cloud rose into the air around them. It was no longer a simple puff of brown dirt; it shimmered gold and burnt umber, with bursts of azure and scarlet. Whimsy took a deep breath, inhaling the swirl of colors that surrounded them until the air was invisible once again.

After a long, quiet moment, Whimsy rose to their feet and said, "I do not understand how a creature such as you could know the tongue of the ancients, but I am grateful to hear them spoken after all these years. Through some strange twist of fate, you have bound us together until such a time as destiny chooses to pull us apart."

"Does this mean you have to do what I say?"

Whimsy shook their head. "Silly human. What you have done is far beyond that. We are now one heart in two bodies."

Ros swallowed back the lump in her throat. "What do you mean? I just wanted you to return the memories of me."

"Instead, you have welded our paths, and we shall not depart this new trail until the world is made right, in whatever plan fate requires of us."

"This is all wrong."

"Perhaps, but it is done all the same."

"What happens now?"

"As you have no life to continue on this side of the curtain—thanks to me, though you still haven't thanked me for my work—we should return to mine and await the unveiling of our new goals."

"Thank you?" Ros asked. "Have you taken leave of your mind? Why would I thank you for ruining my life?"

"Oh, sweet child, you've done enough of that on your own. If anything, I *freed* you from the damage you had already inflicted on yourself."

Ros sighed. "I can't be tied to you, not when you think what you've done was a kindness."

"It's a bit too late for that. You've already linked us."

"Well then, unlink us."

Whimsy slowly shook their head. "That isn't how this works. As you are the one who spoke the words, I would expect you to know that."

Ros gritted her teeth. This was Lucasian's doing. Now she was stuck, bound to this creature, and unsure how to escape. "Fine. What can we do?"

"When hearts are bound as ours are now, the universe always presents a fresh path. All we need to do is walk it."

"Walk the path," she grumbled. "Such helpful directions."

"As I said before, the best thing for us to do is return to my home and allow the path to show itself. It will, I assure you."

"You want me to go into the faerie land? Isn't that dangerous for humans?"

"Very," Whimsy said. "Traversing between worlds has killed your kind, but that is nothing compared to the perils awaiting you in my world."

"If I'm likely to die on the trip or in your world, it seems like a foolish plan. I won't go."

Whimsy smiled, but there was a sadness in their eyes this time. Though they enjoyed their devilish games, Ros sensed there was regret there, too. "You don't have a choice, dear child. When I step through, you will be pulled along with me. By your own words, you have cursed your steps."

"But they weren't my words," Ros whispered to the voice inside her. "You tricked me."

Lucasian said nothing at all.

"Are you ready, then?" Whimsy asked.

Ros watched Whimsy's form flicker in front of her, switching from the tiny Moonchild to the hairy beast. She blinked, unsure what was happening, but then the circle of buds that had been the Night Cradle was suddenly bathed in moonlight and Whimsy solidified in their small form. Ros looked up at the clouds passing overhead, and realized, with a surprising amount of pity, that the poor fae had no control over their own body. They may have magic and power beyond what Ros understood, but they couldn't sustain authority over themselves and they were victim to the whims of the moon itself.

"Is there anything I can say to change your mind and keep you in this world?" she asked.

Whimsy shook their head. "There are strange happenings beyond this plane of existence. I must return to fix what I can, while I can."

"What do you mean?"

"I'm uncertain how to explain it," Whimsy said, tilting their head. "Unrest, perhaps. Change? Maybe. It is more a feeling than a thing. I only noticed it two days past, and still am unsure exactly what *it* is. I was trying to sort it out when your summons came. The only thing for certain is that we are on the precipice of something monumental in my lands, and whatever it is, you are part of it now, human."

With no further explanation, Whimsy stepped forward and disappeared. As soon as they left Rosalinde's world, she felt the pull to follow. It wasn't a desire to go, necessarily, but a *need* deep in her gut. She thought it might be something she could fight if she had some practice. As it currently was, she could do nothing but trip after Whimsy and hope that her passage through the veil was survivable.

She stepped to the place where Whimsy had disappeared, took a deep breath, and closed her eyes. There was a force urging her forward, sure, but there was also a ball of terror writhing inside her. She didn't know what to expect from the world beyond; in the stories, it was full of monsters, and everything on the other side wanted to rip her to bits. But in her experience, the old faerie tales were rarely right.

Her whole heart was here, in this world, and she ached at the thought of leaving. She was desperate to stay and figure out how to save her father, Cassian, her kingdom... but she no longer had a choice. Ros had bound herself to the fae, for good or ill, and the only way she could return to her life was to convince Whimsy to give back the stolen memories and let her return to her world unhindered. She couldn't do that from this side of the veil.

You won't be able to hear me once you step through, Lucasian said.

Ros jolted. She wasn't sure she'd ever get used to having someone else's words in her head, independent of her own thoughts and desires. It was invasive, awkward, and more than a little strange. Though a small part of her was hesitant to leave him behind, more of her was furious with him for what he'd done. She'd finally gotten to the point of offering her trust, and he had instantly betrayed it.

"You were supposed to help me, not trap me with some fae creature."

I am helping, Lucasian thought.

"You lied to me."

Would you have done it if I'd asked nicely?

"Maybe." Ros bit her lip. Of course she wouldn't have. The very idea of it was absurd. Just because his words were true didn't mean his actions were right. "No, I wouldn't have. But I still should have had the opportunity to decide for myself."

You're right. I'm deeply sorry things had to be this way. In time, I hope you will understand my reasons.

"In time?" she asked. A painful lurch in her gut sent her doubling over. The pull to enter Faerie was growing stronger the longer she waited. She forced herself back up, saying, "I'm about to go into another world. Now is the time to make yourself clear."

Lucasian made a vibration in her mind that sounded like a chuckle. *If only it were that easy.*

"Why won't I be able to hear you once I go in?" she asked, hoping he would be less evasive about something he'd already said.

There are mysteries ahead of you, Rosalinde. I cannot answer before they unfold. Though you will not hear me, know that I am with you on this journey.

She rubbed her hands over her face and asked, "Is that supposed to comfort me? A voice in my head who lies to me is promising to always be with me, and I'm supposed to be happy about that?"

Not always with you, he said. *But for now.*

"Why is everything so vague? Just once, I wish someone would tell me exactly what sort of danger I'm facing."

I wish I could reveal your path; truly, I do. But it is hidden, even from me.

"And who are you again? You've never given me a straight answer on that."

Regrettably, I cannot say. Though if all goes to plan, you'll know soon enough.

"What plan? If I knew the plan, maybe I could hurry things along."

Trust only Datura, Lucasian said, ignoring her question.

"Seriously? You want me to trust the fae who got me into this mess?"

You are here for a reason, even if you do not yet understand. Datura is simply the means by which you arrived. Though they are fond of trickery and riddles, they are incapable of lying and they will not harm you.

"You're sure about that? Because I'm not."

Even if they wanted to, they could not. Your connection prevents them from causing you harm.

"At least there's that," Ros mumbled.

Go now, young one. Step through.

"I have so much to do here. You were supposed to help me with that."

Our bargain is not yet met. I will keep my side of it. My word is my bond.

"Your words haven't been worth much."

I tricked you, yes, but I have not lied to you. Continue to trust.

She swallowed. "I'm afraid."

Whatever is waiting on the other side, we'll get through it. And though it means little to you know, that is a promise I freely make.

Ros smoothed her hands down her dress, took a deep breath, and stepped into another world.

Nine

⟡

Walking between worlds reminded Ros of shadow-walking. When she stepped between the shadows, there were bright colors and splashes of light, balanced by thick pools of shadow that seemed like still collections of deep waters. Though space between worlds looked nothing like that, the feeling of stepping from one place to another remained the same. In both instances, she had the distinct feeling she was somewhere she ought not be.

Between her world and Whimsy's, there was rain. It wasn't water, or even liquid, she didn't think, but sparks of sunlight that fell around her in droplets that crackled and fizzled when they hit the ground. The ground! What a sight. It looked like the cerulean sea had been frozen in place, crystallized, and a giant had carved a path through the waves just for her.

The aroma of the in-between was enough to make her want to spend all her days here. Gods below, how could she even describe it? It was the scent of her sister's magic, the feel of silk on bare skin, the hunger in Alaric's kiss, the heat in Cassian's touch. This place smelled like every good thing she'd ever known, every moment she'd ever loved, every tiny thing that had been indescribable until this point. Now those perfect moments were there, flowing around her body like a river, like her magic, and passing through her fingertips like water in a bowl. The descriptions and words that had eluded her for years were as clear as anything had ever been. She breathed deep, smothering her subconscious with love and hope and dreams.

An archway rose in front of her, a door made of wispy purple clouds that shimmered at her approach. She paused, wondering if she *had* to go through it. Could she stay here, surrounded by reminders of all she loved? Could she live on memories for the rest of her days, letting them nourish her until time removed her body from this plane? The thought both delighted and saddened her, for though she would have the sweet memories, she would never again know what it was to be held, or desired, or loved.

She stepped through the door.

As soon as her feet landed in the new world, there was an immediate sense of heaviness that fell on her, as if her body weighed double what it had before. Ros squinted against the harsh light of this strange place, unable to make out anything but a bright haze. She covered her nose and mouth to keep from vomiting from the sour smell that permeated the air and had already somehow coated her tongue with a saccharine aftertaste. A shrill note reverberated through her ears, blocking out all competing sounds. It was all-consuming, an attack on all her senses at once, and nearly unbearable.

She felt a hand—no, a paw—take her by the elbow and lift her up. Ros hadn't realized she was on her knees until then. They led her toward a fire and helped her to sit on a log beside it. The fire was warm, too much so, and a bead of sweat rolled down Rosalinde's forehead. Still, the heat seemed to give her something else to focus on, and all her remaining senses faded into the background. Everything was still too much, but not overpoweringly so.

"All right?" Whimsy said, their voice too high to Rosalinde's ears, too cloying to be pleasing.

"What's wrong with this place?" Ros asked. "It feels too sharp for my senses."

"It's one effect of world-walking," Whimsy said. "The in-between place is so perfect, it makes everything else a cheap imitation. That's why it's so dangerous."

"Dangerous?" Ros repeated. "There was nothing there that could hurt me."

Whimsy sighed, as if they'd had this talk more times than they cared to admit. "How long did it take you to cross?"

"I don't know. Three or four minutes."

"Three days," Whimsy said.

"No," Ros said, a laugh bubbling up in her throat. "That can't be right."

"Few find their way between worlds. Fewer still come out the other side. The danger is not in how that place can harm you, but in how easily it can corrupt your senses and strip you down until there's nothing left of you."

"That's not what it felt like," she said.

"Of course not. No one would stay there if it did."

She watched the sun as it crawled below the mountains in the distance, leaving pale streaks of orange and pink above the darkening horizon. The clouds above were tinted in the final streaks of light, but already beginning to glow a brilliant bluish-white from the moonlight hidden above them. It might have been beautiful if she hadn't just been to the most perfect place imaginable. The hollowness eating away inside her was almost too much to bear. She whispered, "How long will I feel like this?"

"It will fade after a few days."

"You travel through the barrier regularly. How do you deal with it?"

"It lessens over time. Each time you travel through, your visits to that world become shorter as well. I can walk through in seconds now, and the sickness passes within a few hours."

"How many times have you crossed?"

Whimsy shook their head. "Too many to count. I've traveled the worlds since my master first taught me how, and that was nearly two thousand years ago."

Rosalinde's brows rose as she saw Whimsy in a new light. She knew the fae aged differently than humans, that their lives were far extended beyond anything she could imagine, but the idea of being alive for two millennia was too big to wrap her head around.

"I can't imagine..." she trailed off.

"Time is not a concept that comes easy to mortals."

"Are you eternal, then?"

"I can die, if that's what you're asking. Are you planning to murder me?"

"No," she breathed. "I didn't mean—"

"I know what you meant," they said, waving a dismissive hand. "I age, only slower than your kind. For you, I might as well be eternal. But I can be hurt and killed, and if I survive to a natural end, I will live well into my three-thousands."

"What do you do to fill your time? I would grow weary of, well, everything, I think."

"That's a problem for all faeries. We grow bored. And when we are bored, we do stupid things, like make bargains with humans."

Ros smiled despite herself. She wasn't sure why the Moonchild was being so open with her, considering how they had acted toward her previously, but she was thankful to be having a conversation that didn't feel like a battle of wits.

She looked around at the landscape, trying to take in where they were, then inwardly chastising herself for trying to understand a world she'd never seen. It was easy to imagine this was still her world; the mountains in the distance, the rolling hills of heather, a forest not far off. All these things were familiar to her, despite being in Faerie. Even this campfire in the shadow of a green-gray hill seemed like a place she'd been a hundred times.

But there was a strangeness to this place as well. It was as if the very edges of her vision were blurred and tinted in fantastical colors. Whichever way she turned, she got glimpses of vibrant, shifting colors she could never fully see.

After a few minutes, she turned back to Whimsy and asked, "So, now that I'm here, what happens?"

"I do not know. I've only heard camp-side stories about fae who were tied to humans. It is as mythical to me as I am to you."

"Well, what did the stories say?"

"There was usually an epic battle between good and evil that could only be determined by the brave hero-fae and their bumbling human companion that possessed a single thing the hero needed to succeed. Do you possess a thing of value?"

Ros chuckled nervously. "Uh, I'm not sure. It probably depends on the battle."

"Perhaps," Whimsy said. Stroking their chin, they added, "You spoke in the language of the ancients. Clearly, there is something valuable in your head."

She swallowed, thinking of Lucasian. *He* had spoken the voice, not her. She had simply repeated it.

"I know little about the language," she said. "Who are these ancients you keep mentioning?"

"The *Tuath Dé*, the children of the first goddess," they said, as if she should understand. When Ros shook her head, Whimsy continued, "She ruled the worlds in the time *before* time. She created magic and used it to make her children, and once she'd created them, she gave them magic to create that which they desired. Thus the worlds were changed to reflect their hearts, and the lands and waters were filled with creatures to populate them, and after a time, they made us."

"The fae?"

"And the humans."

"Our creation story doesn't speak of the *Tuath Dé*," Ros said.

"That is common in the outer worlds. Some worship the magic used in creation, some attribute only one of the *Tuath Dé* and see them as their god. Some do not recognize their hands at all."

"Outer worlds?" she asked, adjusting her position on the log to be more comfortable.

"Faerie is the center, where all the other worlds connect."

"How many worlds are there?"

Whimsy shrugged. "No one knows. I've been to four, personally, but the old tales lead us to believe there are hundreds."

Yet again, Ros found herself in awe of this new piece of knowledge. Thinking about the fact that she was in a new world right now was enough to send her head spinning. The thought of hundreds of others out there, waiting to be explored? She couldn't fathom it. She hadn't visited every corner of her own world, or even half. There were countries and kingdoms and vast lands she'd never explored, and until this moment she'd never realized how truly unfortunate that was.

"You look tired, Rosalinde Adara Managold."

She smiled. "You don't have to say my full name every time."

"You have given me no other instructions."

"I suppose I haven't," she said. "But it seems we may be together for a while, so you might as well refer to me as my friends do."

"Are we to be friends, then?"

She shrugged. "Better to be tied to a friend than an enemy."

"That is a fair assessment, human."

"Ros. It's better than using my full name and way preferable to *human*."

"But you *are* human."

"I am, but you say it with such disdain."

"I have known many of your kind, *Ros*, and all have been... unpleasant."

"Maybe I'll be the one to change your opinion of us," she said.

"Perhaps," Whimsy said, "but not tonight. You must rest. Tomorrow, we begin our journey."

Ros wanted to ask where they were going and what

they would do, but Whimsy's eyes had taken on a faraway look, and she knew she would get no further with her questions. Instead, she stretched out on the grass, trying not to think about the comfort of her bed at home as she drifted off to sleep.

Ten

Ros awoke to the crackle of fat frying over the campfire. It sounded like the hiss and sizzle of bacon, but the aroma wasn't quite the same. It smelled delicious though, sending her stomach gurgling in protest at her for waiting so long between meals, but it definitely wasn't something she'd eaten before.

Whimsy had their back to her, and she watched them for a long moment without them knowing. She had paid little attention to the details of them before now. Sure, she'd noticed the massive, bear-like body, the coarse fur, the massive claws; she'd been so caught up in the fearful things, and there was far more to them than she'd realized.

Whimsy's fur was mostly black, but it was dappled with hints of blue and brown, the occasional spot of silver. The morning sun caught glints of color, lighting their fur like stained glass. Their paws were more akin to human hands than she'd first thought. Though they were as big as

71

her head, with retractable claws that could shred her in an instant, they somehow looked gentle as they prepared food. Ros had felt that gentleness herself when they had comforted her yesterday.

When Whimsy turned toward her and proffered a large leaf covered in some fried meat, it was only then that Ros noticed the kindness in the fae's eyes. She'd been looking for a beast before, and she'd found it. But when she searched for more, she found that as well.

"It's denock meat," Whimsy said, responding to Rosalinde's unasked question. They returned to the fire for a moment, then reached a paw toward Ros with two small blue eggs cradled in their palm. "And robin eggs."

"I don't know what those things are," Ros said, though she took a helping of each.

Whimsy sat beside her and cracked off the top of their own egg, turning it up like a cup. "Robins are birds like any other, just not one that lives in your world. Denocks are small forest critters that look like a cross between a rabbit and a pig."

Ros tried to picture it, but couldn't. Whimsy swallowed another egg, then put up two fingers on top of their head, like ears. Laughter erupted from Ros at the sight. To see a creature as massive as Whimsy wiggling their hand and scrunching their nose to convey a bunny? It was too much.

When she finally stopped laughing, she asked, "Is it furry like a rabbit?"

Whimsy nodded. "But not as fast as one. Its belly is rounded, and it walks on hooves."

Ros nodded, though she still couldn't imagine the animal Whimsy was describing. She took a bite of the denock meat, her eyes widening at the flavor. "This is delicious."

Whimsy's face lit up, and though Ros wasn't positive, she thought they were blushing. "Thank you. I love to cook, even if it's just a little campfire meal like this."

Ros smiled. It was such a small bit of information from someone who was basically a stranger, but it still made her feel just a tiny bit better about her predicament.

They finished their breakfast in silence, Ros savoring every morsel of the strange food in a strange land. When they were finished, she moved around the campfire to help Whimsy clean up.

"Thanks again for making breakfast," Ros said.

Whimsy's face pinched in a grimace. "About that," they said, pausing in their work to look down at Ros. "I'm going to tell you something very important that will directly contradict what just happened."

"I don't like the sound of that," Ros said, brows furrowing. A worm of anxiety inched its way up through the breakfast in her stomach and she swallowed, trying to erase the tension that had suddenly filled the space around them.

"If a fae offers you food, never eat it. If they offer you a drink, pour it out."

"I don't understand," Ros said. "You're telling me this after I just ate what you offered me?"

"I know. I should have warned you as soon as you stepped into my world, but I was still a little angry with you for binding us together."

"Why are you telling me now?"

"Eating faerie food will make you more susceptible to control."

"Control how?"

"Until the food passes from your system, the fae who spells you can influence you to do their bidding, no matter how dark and vile it might be. You would be powerless to fight against their will."

Ros swallowed the dust that had unexpectedly accumulated on her tongue. "Is that what you just did to me?"

Whimsy's eyes widened. "Do you really think I'd do that?"

"I don't know you," Ros shrugged. "And you *did* remove every hint of my existence from my world, so it doesn't seem that far-fetched."

"That was payment for our bargain, which *you* didn't live up to. It's entirely different."

"It was cruel."

Whimsy pursed their lips. "Perhaps. But a deal is a deal. It isn't my fault that you couldn't keep it."

"You could have done anything else and it wouldn't have hurt as bad as seeing the emptiness in my father's eyes when he looked at me. Especially when I'd only just found him again."

"That was a particularly nasty aspect of the situation." Whimsy scuffed their foot in the dirt. "Still, that isn't the same as what I'm telling you now."

"Cruel and painful for the human involved? Sounds pretty close."

Whimsy balled their fists at their side and, through clenched teeth, said, "I put breadcrumbs on your food this morning."

The words caught Ros off guard. She'd been expecting an explanation of sorts, or anger, maybe something to convince her that Whimsy wasn't the monster she thought they were. But breadcrumbs?

"And? Do you want me to thank you for adding—" she paused, unsure exactly what breadcrumbs were actually *adding* to anything, "—flavor to the food you're going to use to control me?"

"Flavor?" Whimsy asked. The frustration melted from their face, replaced by confusion. "Eat a slice of bread, or even just sprinkle the crumbs on the food you're eating, and no fae can use food or drink against you. Bread prevents the food from being spelled."

"It does?" she asked, chagrined.

"I protected you from myself, for though I had no intention of spelling the food when I awoke this morning, I now see how much easier my life would be if I could control you into shutting your mouth."

The words bit into Ros. Though part of her still believed she was right in her accusations against Whimsy because of what they'd done in her world, another part of her was ashamed at accusing them of poisoning her just as they were starting to get along.

"I'm sorry," Ros said. "I shouldn't have accused you of trying to control me."

"No, you shouldn't have."

"But surely you can see things from my perspective."

Whimsy tossed a vial toward Ros. She caught it against her chest and lifted it to inspect the tan granules within. Breadcrumbs.

"The Fae are not like you, human. We don't see things as you do, we don't feel things as you do, and we certainly don't give a damn whether we harm or help you. You'd do well to remember that while you're here."

Whimsy turned and stomped away, their fur gleaming in the bright morning sun.

Eleven

Ros followed Whimsy in silence for the rest of the morning and the better part of the afternoon. They trudged through high meadow grasses, passed rocky outcrops in the foothills of distant mountains, and stalked through darkened woods Ros would have accused of being haunted if she had anyone she could talk to about them.

Every time she considered breaking their silence to discuss the definitely haunted forests, she got the distinct impression the trees were leaning in a little closer, ready to snatch up her words and use them against her in a very unpleasant way.

Once, she saw an animal scurry across their path as they trudged over upended roots as thick as her waist. Her face lit up when she saw the fuzzy, pointed ears and she turned to Whimsy while she held two crooked fingers above her head. Was this the same creature—a denock, she thought they'd said—that Whimsy had told her about at breakfast? The Moonchild didn't acknowledge her. Ros dropped her hand and her spirits as they continued on.

At some point, when the sun was past the point of being high overhead and was instead creeping onto their backs, they reached a dirt road and followed it. Ros was grateful for it, despite not knowing where it went; where there was a road, there would be people, and hopefully a place to rest.

As the sun drooped lower behind them, Whimsy slowed their pace so that Ros could walk beside them. She had a dozen things flitting through her mind, vying for a chance to make amends with Whimsy, but she wasn't sure if anything she said would matter. As they had said, humans and fae were not the same, so the words that would comfort her could be absolute rubbish to a creature such as them.

Their side-by-side silence continued for a quarter of an hour before Whimsy finally broke it. "There are some things you need to know before we get to town." Ros opened her mouth to speak, but Whimsy pressed on. "I've already warned you about food and drink, but I need to make sure you understand; unless you kill it or harvest it with your own hands, it can be used against you. A sprinkle of crumbs before you eat or drink should keep you safe."

"Should?" she repeated.

Whimsy nodded. "The magic to overpower the bread-crumbs would have to be incredibly strong. One of the *Tuath Dé* could do it, or a High Fae maybe, but none from the lower classes. With luck, we'll meet no one who could put you in danger."

"Aren't I already in danger?"

Whimsy sighed. "No one who will put you in *greater* danger. Just an acceptable amount of danger."

Ros wanted to inquire what level of danger was acceptable, but thought it might frustrate Whimsy into silence again. She wasn't willing to do that since they'd just started talking again.

"Who are the *Tuath Dé*?" she asked instead.

"No one for you to worry about," Whimsy said. "They've been gone for a thousand years."

"That's why you were surprised when I spoke their language."

"One reason, yes. But I'm also surprised anything of theirs made it into the mortal world, much less lasted all these years."

"They were your gods?"

"Not exactly. More like the kings and queens of your world, only far more intoxicating," Whimsy said, taking on a far-off expression. "When they deigned to visit the mortal worlds, then they were like gods; all-powerful, all-consuming beings who could never be known or loved, but humans tried to know and love them all the same."

"Where did they go?"

Whimsy's brow furrowed at her question and the far-off look was replaced by one much closer to pain. "You're awfully interested in them."

"It's the first thing we've spoken about since this morning, when I was an ass."

"Neither of us honored the covenant of our bond today. We must do better to care for one another while we remain connected."

"I want that, too."

"Which is why I need to tell you the rules while I can."

"Never eat or drink faerie food," Ros said. "Got it."

"Do not bow to them, no matter how many titles they string together to sound impressive."

"That's easy. I was raised as a royal. We bowed to no one."

"Not even a curtsy," Whimsy said. "To do so is to admit they have dominion over you. Give that power to no one."

Ros thought back to the night she'd first met Whimsy. "I bowed to you the first night we met."

"And I, you," Whimsy said, "so that neither of us would retain sovereignty over the other."

"You could've had it from the very beginning," Ros said, the realization sending a shiver down her spine.

"In a way, yes, but not as you believe. We were in your world, after all, so none of my control could have been exerted over you there. But had I not bowed, I would have gained dominance once we stepped into this world."

"What can a fae do with dominion over a mortal?"

"Whatever they want," Whimsy mumbled. Then louder: "Mostly they simply use them as servants. A mortal servant is a sign of a prosperous family, since traveling between the worlds is not something all fae can manage. Even less can bring a mortal through."

"So, I guess I shouldn't expect to see many humans here."

"You may see a few, but no matter how friendly they seem or how desperate you are to see another mortal, do not trust them. They are bound to the fae, to their masters, and they will do anything to gain favor, including harming one of their own."

Ros nodded, trying not to let the words dishearten her. Some of these people were surely tricked and trapped in this world, and if she could, she would try to help them. Whimsy's words made it seem as if there was no chance of that.

"Enter no bargains," Whimsy said, oblivious to how their other words had crushed her. "Make no deals or agreements, shake no hands, give your word to no one."

"Yeah, I think I learned my lesson the last time."

"If you think my price high, imagine how much higher it would be from those who are less fond of mortals. And there are many here who despise your kind altogether."

"Good to know," she said. "So, don't eat or drink their food, don't bow, don't bargain, and don't trust other humans. All caught up?"

"Only one more, but it is the most important rule of all: if you see a man with hair of spun gold, with eyes as bright as the morning tide, you must promise to do one thing, and only one thing."

"What?"

"Run. Do not walk, do not hide, do not seek me out—run. As far and as fast as your legs can carry you. Stop for nothing and no one. Once you have run as far as you can, run farther. I will find you and shield you as best as I can."

"I don't understand."

"You don't need to understand, you need to trust me. He is not someone you need to be around, ever. Can you do this?"

"Yes," she said, though the word felt like it was stuck in her throat.

"Good. Remember all these things, for they will save you from what is to come."

"And what exactly is that?"

As the last of the sun faded behind them and the moonlight shone down on Whimsy, Ros watched them transform into the tiny, silver creature she'd seen the first night they'd met. She smiled at them, surprising herself with how delighted she was to see the fae's smaller form.

Whimsy pointed ahead and Ros could see a twinkle of lights and hear a chorus of laughter, though she was certain it had not been there before.

"Get ready, Rosalinde Adara Managold," they said, their small voice finally matching their body again. "Tonight we enter Craicholme, or Carnivaltown, as the humans call it. Hopefully there will still be enough of our bodies and souls remaining when we're ready to leave. But if not, I guarantee we're going to have a helluva good time fading away."

Twelve

From the road where they approached, Carnivaltown seemed like a chaotic mess of buildings, stalls, and shanties. There was no wall or gate to pass through, but as they stepped from the road outside the city to the road inside, Ros could feel a distinct difference in the air around her. She wasn't sure how to explain it, even if only to herself, but she *felt* it; a jittery tingle caressed the very edge of her senses, spreading excitement and chaotic energy across her perception in equal parts.

The sounds of the city surrounded them on all sides. Ros had visited cities before; she had snuck through the darkened streets around Water house, bought trinkets and treats from vendors while in disguise, listened to traveling bards and watched bawdy shows in taverns where she had no business being. None of that had prepared her for this place. It was as if she'd seen a child's version of a city, and now her eyes were open to the real thing.

They walked farther into the city proper. Ros stared up, seeing it was much, much taller than she'd first realized. She couldn't tell exactly how high it went—the town seemed to get lost in the night until she wasn't sure if she was staring at twinkling faerie lights or stars.

Despite the bedlam, magic and beauty suffused the town. Still, something about it bugged her. It wasn't just that it was crowded and noisy and smelly that concerned Ros, but something darker, more sinister seemed to be at play. Along with the strange energy that had met them as soon as they had stepped over the town's boundaries, she felt as if every eye in the place had swiveled to her, if only for a moment. It gave her the creeps.

Whimsy busied themself with business, speaking in a language she didn't understand, despite how familiar it felt to her bones. The words sang to her, called her home. They made her feel alive.

When they stopped for a conversation, Ros took the time to look around the disarray. Ribbons stretched through the air above her head; jewel-toned swathes of cloth dancing through a breeze that seemed to come from nowhere. A tiny figure slid down a sapphire ribbon and careened into a nearby stall. She only worried for a second before the sprite popped back up, laughing.

As they walked through the bazaar, Ros saw every manner of creature she'd read about in fairytale books, and plenty more that she'd never heard of. There were brownies, hobs, and imps playing a dice game she couldn't figure out; goblins, nymphs, and pixies scurried around the market as runners or proprietors of stalls and shops; she saw a nixie, a kelpie, and a phooka, all of which she had to ask Whimsy about.

But it was the human-looking creatures she found the most strange. Sure, some of the other creatures should have impressed her with their tails and horns and wings, but none moved with the same ethereal grace as those she associated in her head with the word "elves."

There were three of them walking down the street, the crowd parting for them and coalescing in their wake. There was something devastating about them, something she couldn't put into words if she tried. Ros knew she would do anything they asked of her, no matter the cost, simply to please them. All were tall, all were beautiful, and all were staring directly at her.

"We need to go," Whimsy said, their voice floating down like a feather through the fog of her mind.

Ros didn't want to go. She wanted to stay and talk to the elves. "But..."

"Stop it," Whimsy said, shaking her arm. She felt something press into her hand and Whimsy said, "Eat this right now."

She felt Whimsy move her arm until her fingers pressed against her lips. She couldn't understand what was so important that they had to ruin this moment by trying to get her to eat... bread? They were feeding her bread? But why?

She nibbled at the crust, trying to remember. Bread was supposed to stop the fae from spelling her with food or drink, but she hadn't had either of them since coming into Craicholme. She took another bite. The fog around her mind lifted a bit, and she suddenly realized the urgency with which Whimsy had spoken as they tried to get her to leave.

"What do we do?" she whispered.

"Nothing," Whimsy said, their eyes tracing the path of the elves as they moved ever closer. "It's too late."

Ros gulped. With her mind clear, she saw them for something far more sinister than she had only moments before. Cruelty lined their smiles, a greedy hunger filled their eyes. They were still beautiful, but also terrible to behold.

"What are they?" she asked.

"Spirits of the Air."

"Like the Air Elementalists in my world."

"Vastly stronger. They're members of the Unseelie Court, just a step below the High Fae. Their mother is the Northern wind. Their fathers are the Fae Guardians of the South, West, and East—protectors of the land. They could suck the air from your lungs and kill you before you could speak a single word of protest."

"I'm scared," she whispered.

"Me, too."

The three members of the Unseelie Court stopped in

front of Rosalinde and Whimsy. She felt the power of their gazes beating down on her, pressing their very will against hers as she met their eyes. It took everything in her not to bow and show deference. Thanks to Whimsy's warnings, she knew not to, but it didn't decrease the urge to do so.

"Are you lost, little human?" the woman on the left asked.

She was easily half a foot taller than Ros, with poker-straight black hair and lightless eyes like pools of midnight. Her skin was made of the night sky—dark, but somehow luminous. Her lips were painted red, and when they parted to show a vicious grin, her entire face shifted from beautiful into predatory.

She felt Whimsy's weight behind her and realized they must've transformed into their other form while the moon slipped behind a cloud. She was grateful. The Moonchild's bulk comforted her, an anchor keeping her from bolting away from the monsters in front of her.

"No, I am exactly where I mean to be," Ros said. She could hear the slight tremor in her voice, but prayed the elves could not. Whimsy hadn't told her how to talk to them; perhaps they hadn't planned on seeing any at the night market.

The woman's grin grew wilder still, but it was the man opposite her who spoke: "Well, well, sister mine, the lamb's teeth are sharper than expected."

"Not sharp enough to gouge, nor strong enough to gash, Corbry."

"But strong enough to cut through your enchantment, Telisa," Corbry sighed. "Whatever shall we do with her?"

"I say we eat her up," Telisa said. She traced her tongue along her incisors.

"You'll not touch a hair on the human's frail head," the middle man said, drawing the eyes of all around. His voice was a deep rumble that Ros could feel down to the soles of her feet.

"Come now, Sulien. Your sour mood is ruining our fun," Telisa said.

"Do you not recognize the changes she brings?" Sulien asked, tipping his head back to take in a deep breath. "Like hurricane winds, this little human is an agent of chaos."

"What do you sense?" Corbry asked, eyes sparkling like stars at the mention of chaos. His likeness to his sister was obvious at a glance; Corbry bore the same glowing dark skin, same black eyes, same long onyx hair, same full smile. But there was an openness about him she did not possess. Though Ros could see the dangers with him as well, he seemed more interested in mischief and disarray versus the violence that lurked just under Telisa's surface.

The brother in the middle, Sulien, was a unique sight altogether. Silver had crept into his hair, though once it may have also been black. His skin, like theirs, seemed to glow as if there were tiny stars implanted under his epidermis, though Sulien's skin was not the same velvety darkness as that of his siblings. He seemed to have a gray pallor to his countenance, and it made Ros wonder if faeries could get sick.

Sulien leaned forward until his eyes, gray-green and luminous, were inches from Rosalinde's. She returned his gaze, willing herself to hold steady. Throughout her life, Ros had out-stared dozens of nobles who intended to intimidate her, had challenged every tutor she'd ever had; she had a backbone of steel when she needed it, and now she needed it more than ever

Whatever he saw in her, a smile spread across his face, though it wasn't the same dangerous one his sister had shown her. No, his smile was almost... pleasant. He took another deep breath through his nose, and she wondered what he was thinking. Was it some sort of fae ritual to torment your prey by sniffing them?

Then, without warning, he jolted back, his eyes full of awe. "Forgive me," he stuttered, dropping to his knee. "I did not recognize you."

A blade flitted to Telisa's fingers, and she flicked her wrist so the metal pressed against Rosalinde's throat. Through gritted teeth, she growled, "What did you do to him?"

"Nothing," Ros stammered.

"Sister, please. Open your eyes. Look past the mortal body and see that which rests within her."

Telisa leaned closer, just as her brother had. Her hair slipped forward, tickling Rosalinde's cheek. Ros dared not move; the woman's blade hovered only a twist away from spraying her blood.

As quickly as the dagger had appeared, it slipped back

into Telisa's cloak as she fell to a knee before Ros, saying, "I did not know."

Corbry didn't bother with the investigation. He joined his brother and sister on the ground before Ros. She stared at the three members of the Unseelie Court, the Spirits of the Air, the most powerful being she'd ever encountered—all bowing at her feet.

Rosalinde's heart hammered wildly in her chest. This wasn't something she and Whimsy had discussed, presumably because it wasn't a scenario the Moonchild had foreseen. Who could have, honestly? Whether they were going to murder her or worship her, she wasn't sure. She didn't like either option, but at least one of them left her breathing.

Whimsy pressed into her side, their fur brushing softly against her arm. "Would someone care to explain what's happening?"

"I'd also like to understand," Corbry said.

Sulien laughed at Whimsy. "As if you don't perceive him already. Your very presence should have told me all I needed to know. The children of the moon are always harbingers of a greater being."

Whimsy's brow creased. They looked to Ros, who shrugged, then back to the elves. "I do not understand—"

"Nor I," Telisa interrupted. "Why would a prince of Faerie put himself at the whim of a mortal? If it is a body you need, take mine, my lord."

Sulien said, "It is not for us to question, merely to

serve. We failed once before; we must make ready their return."

"A prince?" Whimsy asked, seeming to have trouble processing what they were saying. "You're saying—"

"A child of Danu lives inside your mortal girl, Moon-child," Sulien said. "The curse is broken."

Thirteen

⁓

Whimsy ushered Ros through the streets, following in the wake of the Unseelie Court. It all passed in a blur of color and sound as Ros replayed the previous conversation in her head. She knew *someone* had been living in her head, but a faerie prince? It seemed unlikely, impossible even.

Yet...

Part of her felt the truth of it. In her world, Lucasian had always seemed like *more,* even while constricted to her head. He'd been able to bind Whimsy, to speak the language of the old fae. He'd used magic without even having a body. But more than that, the truth of the words seemed to click everything into place. As soon as Sulien had said them, Ros had felt something sing through her, bringing a relief she hadn't felt for a long time.

The surrounding fae of Carnivaltown had not felt the same relief. Though Sulien's words had been conversational and not a loud proclamation, they'd still sent a ripple of whispered panic and quiet fear through the marketplace. Ros wasn't sure why, but it definitely wasn't encouraging.

"You're mistaken," Whimsy had said, their voice rising loud enough for the surrounding crowd to easily hear them. "I've captured a new pet for a family in the east. This little human is nothing more than a bored child's future plaything."

"No," Sulien muttered, brows furrowing.

Corbry had understood the meaning behind Whimsy's words and rose to his feet, pulling his brother to stand beside him. Laughing, Corbry said, "Come, brother, the jest has gone too far. Let's steal the little human and make a meal out of her."

"But Corbry..." Telisa began.

"No arguments, sister. Our good High Ruler would not be pleased if he learned we were making light of the curse. A curse too powerful to be broken, I might add," Corbry said with a chuckle.

Telisa found her feet then. The confusion passed from her face in an instant and she smiled her wicked grin. Scratching one sharp fingernail down Rosalinde's cheek, she said, "Fooled you, didn't we, precious? Fooled you with our silly game, gave you hope for an escape that will never come, and now we're going to eat you!"

"Go with them," Whimsy whispered.

Ros hadn't fully understood what was happening at that moment. The Spirits of the Air's volatile shifts were frightening, and she wasn't sure which aspect of them was their truest personality, or if she'd even glimpsed a moment of truth in their behavior thus far. But she trusted Whimsy and would do as they said, knowing they would protect her as much as they could.

Now, as she rushed through the streets, thinking back on what had happened only moments before, she realized how lucky she was to have Whimsy at her side. It wasn't just their understanding of Faerie and its inhabitants; it was the fact that when everyone else around the market was doing their best to avoid the Unseelie Court, Whimsy had been a solid force at her back. No matter what she faced from here on out, she knew she wouldn't be alone.

So, as the elves walked through the market, parting the other creatures with their presence, Ros and Whimsy followed.

The three siblings led them to a part of town clearly meant for dark dealings. Ros recognized the telltale signs: shabbier buildings, unswept walkways, shady alleyways, and fewer people on the streets. She wondered if they'd gone this way on purpose—they seemed the sort to prefer the fanciest accommodations a place could offer—or perhaps they'd come this way because they'd been in a hurry to get away from any who might still be curious about the show they'd just put on.

The trio approached the doors of a rundown tavern. There was nothing outside to indicate that's what it was, but Ros had no doubt. She could see a cloud of smoke hovering around the place; within twenty paces, she could smell the cheap liquor assaulting her nose with hints of grain, sawdust, and sick. The building itself looked like it would fall over in a strong breeze, despite being wedged between... well, two other dilapidated establishments that didn't look any better.

At the doorway, Corbry turned to her and Whimsy and said, "Wait here." He and his siblings walked inside.

They'd barely been out of sight when Whimsy spun to her. "Did you know?"

"Know what?"

"This isn't the time to play the fool," they said.

She sighed. "I knew there was *something* inside my head. Someone. But I didn't know who."

"You didn't think that was an important thing to share with me, considering we're bonded together?"

"I'm sorry," she said. "Truly, I am. I didn't yet know if I could trust you."

"How long would you have waited to tell me, had we not encountered those who could sense him?"

"I don't know. He hasn't spoken to me since I came through the doorway, so I've felt like I was doing this on my own, despite how you've repeatedly shown me you're worthy of trust."

"He spoke to you? In your world?"

Ros nodded. "A few times when I was in danger. Several more once we arrived in Air house. He's only been in there a few days."

Whimsy chewed on their lip for a moment, a trait Ros often did herself. After a few seconds, they asked, "Do you know his name?"

"Yes."

A commotion at the tavern pulled their gazes to the doorway. Several fae were pushing their way out, stumbling over one another in a rush to get away from the woman at their backs. Telisa. She certainly had an effect on people, and it never seemed to be positive.

"Let's go, human," she called, loud enough to throw off anyone who might be listening. "I'm starving, and you look delicious."

Ros and Whimsy followed Telisa into the tavern. Though the inside fared little better than the outside—dirty tables perched on sagging floorboards, dingy mismatched fabric for curtains, an odor that could stun a mule at fifteen paces—a pristine hearth warmed the room with its blazing fire and gave out enough light to make the place look as homey as possible, given the circumstances.

Corbry and Sulien were seated at the table directly in front of the fire; though every table in the place was empty, theirs was the only one that looked clean enough to use. Telisa, Whimsy, and Ros joined the brothers at the table.

As soon as they sat, Corbry smiled brightly and waved over a fae creature, who looked remarkably like a toad. Their skin was a mottled yellowish-brown, flecked with black and orange. Their eyes were bulbous things, perched on the sides of a slitted nose and flat, featureless lips.

"Good evening, Anura. Pleasure to see you, my good man. Apologies for clearing out the rest of your clients."

"No apologies needed," Anura said. "Your presence is

always a treat. And you always order more than a dozen of my other patrons combined!"

Anura's voice was lighter than Ros expected, more a chirp than anything else. It took her a second to catch the rhythm of his words, but once she did, she found his cadence quite soothing.

"What can I say? Your fare is the best in the land, and I strive to fill my belly to the brim to sustain me until my next visit."

Anura smiled. "You're too kind."

"Let's begin this evening with a round of your finest drinks for my companions," Corbry said. "Anything extra tasty on the menu tonight?"

"Rumor is you're eating the mortal. She can be cooked in several ways that might please you, but it will take some time to prepare her."

Corbry laughed. "You know how rumors fly around here. Nothing is ever as it seems."

"So you're *not* eating her? Is that because she's really a long-lost prince?" Anura asked.

"No, it's because I'm a vegetarian," Telisa growled.

Anura swallowed, clearly nervous at the sister's attention. Corbry simply laughed again, drawing the fae's eyes back to him. "Pay her no mind. We'll have the stew—all of it. Whatever fruit you have on hand. Do you have any eggs?" Anura nodded and Corbry continued, "Wonderful. I love all of your egg dishes, so feel free to surprise me." He tapped a finger against his chin and said, "What else, what else? Ah yes, a hunk of brown bread for the girl, if you have it. Lots of butter. Cheeses—stars, please, all the cheeses. One of your husband's pies, doesn't matter the flavor. And for Telisa," he said, shooting her a grin, "a potato."

The toad hurried off to the kitchen and Corbry turned back to the table. Ros had been watching him the whole time he ordered, looking for a hint of the malice she'd seen in his sister, but there was none to behold. Then again, perhaps he was unwilling to show it to the girl with a prince in her brain.

Corbry smiled when he caught her watching him. Ros tried to avert her gaze, but he said, "No, please, stare at your leisure. I'm fully aware of my undeniable beauty, and the way it draws even the most unwilling eye. Besides, there's nothing I like more than an audience."

"Except tormenting humans on the street?"

The words had slipped out faster than she could control them, but Corbry's smile didn't waiver. He leaned toward his siblings and said, "You know, I like that she isn't afraid of us. Or at least not as afraid as they normally are. It makes these exchanges a tad more exciting."

"If she isn't afraid, it's because she doesn't know better," Whimsy said.

Telisa nodded. "Now that she knows we aim to serve the prince inside her, she's assured safety. For now."

Anura returned with multiple platters of food while a smaller version of himself trailed behind with a tray of drinks. The platter trembled in the child's hands, and Ros saw fear in their eyes as they approached.

"Steady, lad," Anura murmured. "They'll not hurt

you. Our tavern is a friend of the Unseelie Court. You know that."

"Yes, Papa," the boy squeaked.

"Your father is right, little one," Corbry said, his tone no longer jovial, but gentle. "I pledge to you right now, I will never harm a spot on your head, nor your father's, nor whomever comes next in your line."

The boy's eyes flitted around the table, lingering a moment on Telisa. Everyone else at the table followed his gaze. She pressed her lips in a tight line for a moment, but finally said, "Fine. I give the same oath as my little brother."

Ros watched the exchange with a strange fascination. It wasn't just that there was a break in the malice from before, there was actual kindness here. From Corbry, at least. He was clearly the moral compass of the group, or at least a deterrent from evil for Telisa. Like all families who loved one another, she wanted to see her brother happy.

Rosalinde's eyes moved to Sulien. He'd been silent since Corbry had pulled him to his feet in the market. When she caught his gaze, she wondered if he'd taken his eyes from her since they'd entered the tavern. They certainly were boring into her now.

Once the toads were out of earshot, Sulien said, "Tell us who you are."

"My name is—"

"No," Whimsy said, holding up a paw. "They have no need of your name."

Telisa smiled her wicked grin. "I don't *need* it, but I'd certainly enjoy having it."

"There's power in names," Corbry said around a mouthful of yellow cheese. "On this side of the veil, we can control you if we know your full name. On your side, vice versa. It is why we often have two names—one for strangers, and our true names for those who love and guard us."

That was a rule Whimsy hadn't told her, though they had stopped her from giving it. Perhaps they hadn't thought her foolish enough to blurt it out to anyone who asked. When she thought about it, perhaps *they* were the foolish one. She had given it to them the night they'd first met.

Corbry pushed a plate across the table toward her. There was a shallow bowl of stew with chunks of root vegetables peeking over a thick reddish broth with swirls of pale cream. Beside the stew was a dense brown bread still warm from the oven, a dollop of yellow butter melting on top. The food was far plainer than she'd imagined faerie food. She'd expected precarious towers of spun sugar and ornate bowls that glowed and glittered with their contents; instead, she found herself thinking of the millers and farmers and bakers back home.

A finger of steam lifted from the bowl of stew, beckoning her closer. She leaned over and took a deep breath; the aroma sent a rumble through her stomach.

Corbry slid a flagon toward her. He swallowed another mouthful of cheese and asked, "You know about the bread?"

"Of course she does," Whimsy said. "She's not completely hopeless."

Corbry smiled, shrugged, and popped another piece of cheese in his mouth, watching as Ros scraped some bread-crumbs into her hand. "You know," he said, "you don't have to put the crumbs in if you just eat the bread first."

Ros looked from him to Whimsy, and Whimsy nodded. "It's true. As long as you eat the bread intermittently with the food, it works the same. I didn't expect you to have bread so readily available. Most fae avoid it."

"I'm not most fae," Corbry shrugged.

Sulien leaned forward and said, "Can we get back to the discussion at hand? I don't care what you eat or who *you* are, human; I want to know which prince has returned from the cursed tomb."

Ros turned to Whimsy to make sure she should say, but their eyes were locked on her the same as everyone else's. She took a deep breath and said, "Lucasian."

There was a moment of stunned silence where Corbry even stopped chewing. Finally, Sulien whispered, "The very Night himself. Our Prince of Shadows has returned."

Fourteen

C onversation swirled around Rosalinde as she dug into the bread, then the rest of the food. She tried to follow their words, but once the fae heard Lucasian's name, their talking became more animated, faster, and overlapping. Ros found it easier to focus on filling her hungry stomach than on the jumble of words bombarding her ears.

Once she'd had her fill of bread and stew, she considered trying to resume the conversation with the others, but found they were speaking of people and events so long ago, she couldn't fathom the amount of time that had passed between then and now. She pushed her chair back from the table, stood, and when no one objected or even seemed to notice that she was excusing herself, she moved to the small chaise lounge on the other side of the hearth. The heat of the fire, combined with the warm food in her belly, had her dozing in mere minutes.

A while later—minutes, hours, she didn't know—Corbry roused her from her sleep as he sat on the floor next to her, proffering a piece of pie for each of them. By the time she forced her mind awake, Corbry had eaten a couple bites, smiling at her with teeth stained a violent shade of purple.

Ros laughed. "The color suits you."

"Every color suits me." He wagged his brows.

She rolled her eyes. "A bit cocky, aren't you?"

"Confident," he said, taking another bite.

Ros scooped a forkful toward her mouth, but before it hit her lips, Whimsy called out, "Bread, girl!"

She'd had bread not long before. But no, Whimsy had said she had to eat it along with the food. All the rules were getting mixed up in her sleepy brain.

She looked from Whimsy to Corbry. His smile was more pronounced, devious, but something about his expression made her certain he hadn't meant her any actual harm. Perhaps that was what he was counting on; looking harmless was a handy trick, fae or not.

"Don't look at me like that," Corbry said, putting on a pout when she leveled her gaze at him. "It's a lesson you must learn. Better to do so in the presence of friends."

"Friends? Earlier you were talking about eating me," Ros said.

"It's still not off the table," he shrugged. He finished his pie and reached his fork toward her plate, stealing a nibble of the crust before she could stop him. "Pass it over if you don't want it. Ouluma pie is my favorite."

"I thought blackberry was your favorite," Telisa said.

Ros jolted at the closeness of her voice. The woman was standing just behind them, but Ros hadn't heard her approach. *A perk of being fae*, she thought.

"That was last week," Corbry said. "This week, I'm into Ouluma."

"You're into whatever Anura's husband has ready when you show up unannounced."

Corbry shrugged. "That man can make a damn good pie."

"Well, finish your meal. We're about to leave."

"Where are we going?" Ros asked.

Telisa looked down at her. Ros could tell she was doing her best not to sneer at her, and half-succeeding. Ros might have a prince in her head, but it didn't make Telisa hate humans any less.

"The tomb. It's time we figure out how to get Lucasian out of your head and into our world."

THE NIGHT OUTSIDE had turned cold, or maybe it was the warmth she was leaving behind, and Rosalinde's teeth started chattering as soon as they left the tavern.

"Poor thing," Corbry said. "We should get you something warmer to wear."

"I don't have any money."

"That's fine," he said, his lips curling into a winning smile. "I'll make you a deal—"

"No," she and Whimsy said at the same time.

"You haven't even heard my proposition."

"I don't need to," she said. "I will make no bargains with the fae."

"At least you've taught her that much," Telisa said as she pushed past them into the street.

"How much can you teach a babe?" Sulien asked. Though he spoke to her, or at least about her, Sulien's eyes were cast to a faraway place.

Telisa spun back to face them. "So, how are we going to do this?"

"I'll take her," Sulien said.

"Not alone," Whimsy said.

"You'll not be far behind. My family will carry you."

"Can you switch to your other form, though?" Corbry asked. "I'd much rather carry a mini-Moonchild than—" he paused, waving his hand in front of Whimsy's midsection "—this."

"I can't change form without the moon, and you know that. It wouldn't matter, anyway. My weight is the same, no matter which form I'm in."

"I have a difficult time believing that."

"You're wasting time," Sulien said, his voice suddenly commanding and his expression fully present. "Our Prince of Shadows has waited long enough."

Whimsy grabbed Rosalinde's arm, their claws digging into the flesh of her forearm. They bent their head low and in a furious whisper, said, "I will come for you. I will always come, no matter what happens. Do not fear. Make no deals. Trust no one."

"Calm down," Corbry said, sidling up between them. "My brother wouldn't dare cross Prince Lucasian on the eve of his return."

Ros saw in Corbry's face that he truly believed his words, but she could see the opposite in the crease of Whimsy's brow. Whatever they'd discussed while she dozed had done little to convince the Moonchild that the Unseelie Court was allied with them.

Sulien reached a hand toward Rosalinde, and when she nodded her consent, he stepped toward her. Her hand slipped into his, and in an instant, they were gone.

TRAVELING with the Spirit of the Air was nothing like shadow-walking, though it was the only thing Ros could think to compare it to. Rather than stepping from one shadow, one place, to another, Sulien seemed to glide through the air with giant leaps. Their feet didn't touch the ground as they moved, hovering a few inches above it instead.

They rushed toward their destination with a speed Ros couldn't quite register. A blink and they were out of Carnivaltown, another and they were passing the road where Whimsy had warned her of the rules she'd need to remember around the very figure who held her now.

The world blurred by for several minutes as they sailed

past lands she'd never know and places she may never see again. When Sulien pulled them to an abrupt stop, the food in Rosalinde's stomach gurgled up and she turned her head to puke in the same spot where she'd sat that morning at breakfast. After the contents of her gut had emptied onto the ground, she wiped her mouth and turned back to Sulien, embarrassed.

Ros was surprised to see him wincing as he watched her. "Apologies, young one. Traveling by wind is fast, but imprecise, and stopping is often abrupt. I should have been gentler with you. It's been many years since I've spent time with a human, and it seems I've forgotten some of their more delicate sensibilities."

She pursed her lips. While she appreciated his apology, he also seemed to call her weak in the same breath. In comparison, though, she was.

"I'm fine," she said. Then, wondering if she could get some information from him while he was repentant, she asked, "Who was the last human you were around?"

A flicker of pain crossed his face, gone as quick as it came. He held out his arm for her to take it, much like a gentleman in her own world offering a walk. She took it and they started walking toward the hill ahead.

"He wasn't from your world, but another place ours connects to, called London."

"A long time ago?"

Sulien nodded. "Two-hundred and forty-six years."

"I can't imagine."

"None of your kind can. It isn't a detriment, mind you,

but a beautiful trait that my people see as a flaw. Our lives are too long to grasp the same level of passion that your brief years offer you."

"But you have so much time to figure out what you care about."

"Too long," he said. "Most of the time, we find ourselves not caring about anything. There's no point in having a fire in your bones for a thousand years. Time is an expanse that some cannot cross. Humans, though, you burn brightly for a century and die out with a heart still aflame. It's astonishing."

"You loved him."

Sulien patted her hand as it rested in the crook of his arm. "You've taken minutes to understand what my brother and sister have yet to see."

"How could they not?" Ros asked. "Your face says it all."

"They do not see it because they do not want to. The thought of me, son of the Northern Wind and the Guardian of the Southern realm, in love with a mortal? And not just a mortal, but a *human*."

"We're not so bad," Ros teased.

"So I've learned. Edmundo taught me much about your kind, the beauty and love you're capable of. I must admit, I hadn't thought of those things for a long time. Until I came face to face with you tonight, actually. You remind me of him a bit; indeed, you have the same fire."

"It also helps that I've got a long-lost prince in my head."

Sulien laughed, a booming, joyous thing. "It definitely made it easier to convince Telisa. But I assure you, I had no intention of letting her hurt you."

"And Corbry?"

"He likes to play the part of the dangerous fae, especially in my sister's company, but he's mostly harmless. I can't promise he won't *try* to gain control of you—it's his favorite part of playing with humans—but he wouldn't intentionally cause harm. He's only interested in the entertainment of it all."

Ros pressed her lips tight, trying not to say the multitude of things running through her head. Being a faerie's pet was far from a good life, and she had no intention of letting anyone play with her for entertainment. But she held her tongue, not wanting to stop the flow of conversation since Sulien had been so pleasant and forthcoming.

The seconds ticked by while she worked to control her reaction, and in that time, the others arrived at the campsite below them. Ros heard a peel of laughter and turned to see Corbry pointing at the firepit where she'd puked.

As she and Sulien watched them climb the hill, he said, "I would appreciate it if you said nothing about what we discussed. Compassion is not a trait you'll find in my siblings, even toward their own brother and his lost love."

"You have my word," she said. She laced her fingers through his and gave a gentle squeeze of assurance.

"Looks like you've gotten chummy," Corbry said as the trio reached them. "I don't know that I'd go much further than holding hands, though, considering what recently departed her mouth."

"Very funny," Ros said.

"Get it out now," Telisa said. "You won't be making jokes when we're with the Prince of Shadows."

Corbry's brows knit together. "Are you sure? I honestly can't remember a damn thing about him. Maybe he was the funny one."

"No, that was Mallory," Telisa said. "Lucasian was the broody one."

"Oh, good," Corbry mumbled. "Like we don't have enough of that with Sulien around."

Sulien shot a glance back to his siblings, sending them both into silence, then turned to Ros and asked, "Ready?"

"As ready as I can be," she said. "Let's get this guy out of my head."

Fifteen

They crested the hill. Ros had expected something grand on the other side; the prestigious tomb of a fae prince would surely be ornately decorated, ostentatious even. Instead, there was... nothing. It was just a hill. There was a circle on the ground of black charred earth, a circle that reminded her of...

"The Night Cradle," she said.

"What?" Sulien asked.

"It's a place in my world," she said, "a source of power. It's the point where Night magic is the strongest in my world."

Whimsy nodded. "The veil is thin there. When they entombed Lucasian here, they must have used parallel points in the other worlds to anchor him."

"I always wondered how they did it," Sulien said. "The princes held such power. It never made sense that they could be locked away so casually."

111

"I broke the hold," Ros said.

Sulien's brow creased into a crumpled line. "How so?"

"The anchor in my world was leaking magic. I sensed it, but didn't really know what I was doing. I absorbed the magic and told the force that it could share my body. I didn't know exactly what it meant to do so, but I could feel it was the right thing. It must've been Lucasian I felt pouring through the anchor, and Lucasian who wound his way into my brain."

"By letting him share your mind, the hold the tomb had over him was weakened. He was free to roam outside this place and regain his strength," Sulien said.

"We're making a lot of assumptions," Whimsy cut in. "We should probably go inside and let him tell us what happened instead of guessing."

"Inside where?"

Whimsy pointed at Rosalinde's feet. She looked down, surprised to see a faint golden circle cut into the blackened dirt. "The tomb can only be opened by one of the *Tuath Dé*, but they were all entombed, creating a curse that couldn't be broken."

"But a piece of the *Tuath Dé* is inside you," Sulien said. "If you command the tomb to open, it will."

Ros nodded, took a deep breath, and spoke the first words that came into her mind: "Open wide your golden doors that I may enter this unholy place."

She didn't know *why* she'd said those words, and those around her seemed to glance at one another, also unsure.

Still, she had that same rightness in her bones as when she'd first discovered who was in her head.

"What did you say, human?" Telisa asked.

Ros furrowed her brows. "You didn't hear me?"

Telisa pursed her lips. "I haven't heard the spoken words of the *Tuath Dé* for a thousand years, and thought I never would again. Much of their language now escapes me."

She had spoken another language without realizing it? Perhaps Lucasian's influence was still stronger than she realized.

Ros opened her mouth to explain to them what she'd said, but before she could say a word the ground below her feet vibrated, soil and rocks shaking over and around her feet. Without warning, a crack formed under Rosalinde's body and she dropped into the open space. She landed hard. It took her a stunned second to realize she was fine, aside from a scratched palm and a tinge in her ankle.

She looked around. Ros was in an arched chamber of copper, gold, and thick-veined blue marble. There were symbols carved into the upper portions of the room; rather than the ornate metals throughout the rest of the place, these carvings seemed to be made of something much duller—iron, if she were to guess.

She looked for the crack she'd fallen through, but the ceiling appeared flawless, with no hint of where she'd entered. Her heart hitched at the next realization to hit her: she was entirely alone.

A slight panic roved up her chest, a heaviness that

pressed on her and made it hard to breathe. She had fallen into a locked tomb that could only be entered by the people inside. Now that she was here, could she get out?

She pressed her hands against the cold marble floor and pushed herself up. Pain shot through her ankle when she tried to put weight on it, letting her know she had indeed sprained it. What she wouldn't give for a big burly Elementalist to carry her right now! But the days of the Great Match and her short time in it seemed like a lifetime ago, though in reality it had only been a bit over a month. How had so much happened in such a short time?

Ros took a deep breath, shoving aside thoughts of home. She couldn't do anything for the people there while she was trapped in a tomb in another world. If she wanted to see her father and sister, her best friend, Larkin... if she wanted to see *Cassian* again...

She surveyed the room, looking for a way out. The area where she'd fallen seemed almost like a bridge separating one doorway from another. On each side was a pool of crystalline liquid. Water, perhaps. Behind her, the door was opulent gold with mother-of-pearl inlay. There was an intertwined couple depicted vividly upon it, in a position Ros knew was more than impossible. Or, as she studied it further, very, very difficult without being inhumanly flexible.

Ahead were steps leading to another door—plain gray and unadorned. She forced herself forward, hobbling on her injured ankle. Ros pushed herself up the steps, holding onto the marble columns for support. She placed her hands on the blank slab and, not seeing a way to move it, she simply said, "Open."

The door slid out of her way and Ros passed through the entryway into the antechamber. On each side of the room were doors to smaller rooms. Some were open, some closed, but there was nothing in any of them that would pull her attention away from what was in front of her. At the end of the room, in a gold throne that forked above his head like vast tree branches, sat the man she had come to free: the Prince of Shadows, the very Night himself, Lucasian of the *Tuath Dé*.

Sixteen

H e was stunning. As if he radiated his own light, a faintly glowing aura surrounded him, proving his divinity. Thick honey-gold hair seemed to reflect sunshine, despite the sun having no way to shine into this underground tomb. His jaw—was it actually made of diamond? No, of course not, but it certainly looked as if it could cut like one. His eyes were violet, growing darker at the outside of his irises, and holding a strange curiosity in them as he looked at her.

And he *was* looking at her.

Ros felt heat rising up her chest, her neck, into her cheeks and the tips of her ears. His eyes seem to roam everywhere the color tinged. She felt exposed, yet strangely seen, like no one else had ever looked as deeply into her as Lucasian was at that very moment.

"I thought you'd have dark hair," he said, his perfectly shaped brows furrowing.

A giggle escaped Rosalinde's lips. She couldn't help herself. Of all the things she expected him to say, that wasn't one of them. Ros delivered an unexpected line of her own: "I thought you'd be better looking."

"I am a specimen of beauty and perfection, the likes of which you've never seen. We both know it."

There was no laughter in his face at that, nothing to indicate he was joking. He'd said it matter-of-factly, and because he himself had told her that the fae were incapable of lying, she knew he believed his words as truth.

What an ass.

"And so modest, too."

"How long is appropriate to continue this charade before we move on?" he asked. "We have business to discuss."

Ros ground her teeth together. She knew she should be polite and give her best courtly manners, but something about this man irked her far beyond the point of being polite. She'd been tolerant of him when she didn't have to look at him, but something about having him stand there and act that way really bothered her, considering his only path to freedom was through her.

"Oh, is this the part where you tell me why you've been hitching a ride in my head?"

His eye twitched ever so slightly as he said, "You could ask me anything, learn the secrets of the worlds, and that is what you most desire to know?"

"It's important, whether or not you want to admit it."

"Yes, there is a sliver of myself, barely worth mentioning, stuck inside you. I want it back."

"Is that why you tricked me into coming here?"

He gave a terse nod. "I regret it had to be done that way. But once you return what is mine, you're free to go."

A thought crept through her mind, and before she could stop herself, she said, "That wasn't our bargain."

"Your task is complete."

"Maybe so, but our bargain was for ten days. I only left my world four days ago."

"Only four? I thought the in-between would take you longer to cross."

"Three days," she said, "though it felt like minutes. Then traveling with Whimsy for a day."

He lifted his face toward the ceiling as if looking at something she couldn't see. "Dawn is breaking on the fifth day, but once you return me to fullness, your side of the deal is finished."

"And yet, our bargain is not met."

A sound emanated from his throat, somewhere between a growl and a sigh. "I will do that which I've promised. You have my word."

"I have no doubt of it. Still, I will finish my time with you."

"Why are you so adamant about staying in Faerie? Do you not comprehend the dangers of remaining in a world that is not your own?"

"I understand. But I'm also fully aware of the dangers of breaking a deal with a fae. You may say my part is complete, and you may even be sincere, but our agreement was for ten days—no more, no less."

He raised his brows as his lips twisted into a smirk. "At least you have learned *something* while you've been here. It may not benefit me, but I am pleased to see a human take the faerie bargain with the seriousness it deserves."

There was a moment of quiet while the two surveyed each other, weighing the other's worth. Finally, Ros broke it, saying, "And what if I decide not to return this part of you?"

"Why would you say such a thing? Of course you'll return it."

"I don't know. I mean, having you in my head has been a nuisance, but you've also been helpful. Maybe I want to keep the knowledge that only a *Tuath Dé* can give me." His eyes shot up, holding her in place, but she fought to keep her voice normal as she added, "Don't look so surprised. It was easy to work out, and the Unseelie Court confirmed it once they got involved."

"The Unseelie..." he muttered, trailing off. A second later, he asked, "Which of them are involved?"

"Sulien, Corbry, and Telisa. You didn't know?"

He shook his head. "I haven't been able to use your eyes since we crossed the veil."

"Why?"

He waved away her question like a gnat, focusing on the elves instead. "How did they get involved? Did you strike a bargain with any of them?"

"They found us in Craicholme. They *saw* you in me. And no, I didn't strike any deals."

Lucasian stroked his chin for a moment, as if thinking over what she had said. She thought he muttered Sulien's name, but the sound was so soft, she wasn't sure she hadn't imagined it. He crossed his arms over his chest and she thought he would say more about the siblings, but instead he returned to his original train of thought: "I'm willing to purchase what belongs to me. What do you want in exchange?"

She met his gaze, staring into his strange violet eyes. Ros knew exactly what she wanted, but she didn't want to seem too eager. "I could ask for riches?"

"I would give them."

"Or a deep and abiding love?"

"It shall be done."

"Perhaps I should ask for revenge against my enemies."

His expression grew dark. "I will wreak havoc on them."

She shivered at his words, realizing she might be pressing him in the wrong direction. She decided it was time to ask for what she really wanted. "I want to be restored in my world. I want to be remembered."

Lucasian pressed his lips into a grim line, swallowed. "That is the one thing I cannot do."

"You can give me anything else, anything I ask for, except the one thing I truly want?"

"I cannot restore that which I did not take."

"Fine. Force Whimsy to give the memories back."

"Datura serves me at their own discretion. I do not command them. Your bargain, and your debt, is with them."

Ros felt sick to her stomach. She thought this was her way out. Instead, she was again faced with a fae who couldn't—or wouldn't—help her, and no way to fix the thing that mattered most. She wanted to scream, to rage at Lucasian and Whimsy and anyone else who would listen. But it was pointless. Instead, she would use this boon to benefit her in another way. She wouldn't let it go to waste like her bargain with Whimsy.

"I will accept another reward."

"Name it."

"Free my father and Cassian and get them to safety. They will be safeguarded and well cared for, out of reach from anyone who wishes them harm."

Lucasian stared up at her. "You trust me to do that?"

"The *Tuath Dé* have more magic than they know what to do with," she said. She hoped he couldn't see her lack of confidence in her own words, or the way she was gambling with something she didn't fully understand.

"Alas, I am not whole. Part of me is still trapped inside that mind of yours."

Ros folded her arms across her chest. "If you want it back, you'll figure something out."

His mouth changed from a flat line into a broad smile, lighting up his face in such a way that she found him hard to look at. He was painfully beautiful, a sight too grand for mortal eyes. Though she wanted to look away, she refused to grant him the satisfaction. These creatures thought her a weak mortal girl, and maybe, compared to them, she was. Still, she would show them in every small way, every tiny act of defiance, that she was more than they expected.

"Done."

Her brows rose. "Just like that?"

He nodded. "I'll send my best warriors to protect them, with their very lives, if necessary."

"Do you have warriors, or anyone, really? Whimsy says you've been locked away for a thousand years. How many of your servants remain?"

Ros felt guilty for her words when his smile faded. "A thousand years to the fae is not as long as it is to a mortal. Still, I worry about what has become of those who served me. Strahn is not known for his kindness."

"Who is Strahn?" she asked.

"He's the villain of my tale, the reason I was locked away this last millenia."

Ros gave up her plans of standing through the entire conversation and plopped down on the cold marble. Taking her cue, Lucasian moved to sit beside her. She asked, "What happened?"

"It's a long story."

"I've got time."

"It would take a hundred years to tell the whole thing."

"Maybe just a summary, then."

He chuckled and said, "Strahn was my... friend. Or at least, I considered him as such. He was born into the Unseelie Court, whereas my family ruled the Seelie."

"Is he another sibling of the elves waiting outside?"

"Elves?" he asked.

She shrugged. "That's the easiest way for me to think of them."

"No, he isn't related to them, nor to the other two you haven't met—Penrose and Sarokia."

"There are more like them? Three seems like enough to handle."

Lucasian smiled. "They can be a challenging bunch, for mortals especially. All five together are fierce and formidable."

Ros shuddered. "I can't imagine." Then, returning to the core of his story, she asked, "So, how did you become friends with Strahn?"

"We met as children and I was fond of him immediately. Many believed our friendship would one day unite the Courts, though I never gave thoughts like that much weight. I gave nothing much weight, if I'm being honest."

"Has that changed?"

Lucasian nodded. "My mind was awakened during my confinement, Rosalinde. For the past thousand years, there was nothing to do but think about the things I've done wrong. My disregard for the wellbeing of my people in favor of frivolous delights, well, that was the thing I regretted the most."

"Not your friendship with Strahn?" she asked.

"No. I wish I could hate him for what he did, but it is not in me to feel such things. I regret I could not be the friend he needed, that somewhere through the years, he began to see me as a rival. If I could go back in time and find the source for whatever pain turned him against me, I would. Unfortunately, I was unaware of those feelings and oblivious to his intentions until it was too late."

"What did he do?"

"Strahn somehow convinced the nobility of both Courts that my family should be removed from power. Even after all these years, I cannot fathom how he managed it. Once he did, they banded together and used powerful, old magic to contain us within the barrows—Cradles, as you call them—binding us in our world and yours, rendering our magic useless."

Ros furrowed her brows. "Wait, what do you mean? I've seen fae do magic in my world."

"Lesser fae, certainly, but not the *Tuath Dé*. When the worlds were split, we struck a bargain that the High Fae could never use their powers in your world."

"But I watched *you* use magic."

"No, I simply tapped into the magic you already possessed."

Ros felt as if her head was spinning. Each new bit of information Lucasian doled out made her more confused than the one before. One thing stuck out, stranger than the rest, and she asked, "When the worlds were split?"

He smiled, and this time she saw a kindness there that she hadn't seen before. "There was a single line about it in the books we read. I fear there is more history in my short story than in all the books of your library."

"Feels that way," she said around a yawn.

"You've had a long day. Several long days, in fact, and I need you whole before I take back the part of me that resides in you," Lucasian said. "We can speak more of this later, after you've rested."

Ros wanted to protest, to find out as much as she could while he was being talkative instead of infuriatingly vague, but her body didn't have the same need for answers. Instead, she nodded and moved to lie down on the floor. Her eyes were already closed when she felt Lucasian's thick arms lift her. He carried her into a smaller room and placed her on the softest thing her body had ever touched. Seconds later, she drifted off to her dreams.

Seventeen

R os awoke to the sound of singing. The dirge echoed through the antechamber and into the side room where she'd been sleeping. The tone was so forlorn, so hopelessly mournful, she didn't need to comprehend the words to understand the pain. It was no surprise to her when she felt the tear roll down her cheek, and even as she wiped it away, another took its place.

The voice was almost unbearably beautiful in a way that made her think of her mother, solemn in a way that reminded her of her father, nearly as wild as her sister. But it was the brokenness that she could hear in every note that resonated most with her; it was the words of her kingdom, the tears of Talabrih, the voice that the magicless people didn't have, infused with the pain that had gone unrecognized for centuries.

She stood, willing her body to be silent and her movements to be stealthy, as she tiptoed to the door. A nervous flutter bounced through Rosalinde's chest as she stepped closer to the rise and fall of the notes. Though Ros knew there was only one person the voice could belong to—he'd been the only one in these chambers for a thousand years—she still found herself surprised when she saw Lucasian.

He meandered around the outer edge of the antechamber, a slow, methodical path he'd probably walked a million times. He was bare to the waist, his muscles gleaming from a light source she couldn't trace. Or, possibly, he was the light.

When he turned at the corner of the room to walk down the side where her room was, he looked up and saw her watching him. His song stopped immediately, as did his steps, and Ros was certain embarrassment flashed across his features, as if he'd forgotten her presence altogether until this moment. It lasted only a second, quickly replaced with a hard look she couldn't quite read.

He closed the distance between them in slow, unsure steps, saying, "I apologize if I woke you. I often pass my time wandering this place."

"No, please, don't apologize," she said. "It was lovely."

The corner of his mouth twisted as if he wanted to smile, as if he was relieved at her response; instead, he straightened his face, cleared his throat, and asked, "Did you sleep well?"

"I did, thank you. How long did I sleep?"

"A few hours. Long enough for the others to worry, I'm sure. No effects from Datura being too far away?"

Ros shook her head. She'd only felt the aching pain of

separation from Whimsy when they had stepped into Faerie without her, but that one time was something she would not forget for a long time.

"That's good. They must be nearby, hoping you'll find a way back to them."

"Will I?" she asked. The thought had been niggling at her brain since she got there. Would the curse stop them from escaping now that all the *Tuath Dé* was returned to the tomb? Or, worse yet, what if transferring Lucasian's final piece shattered her? Could returning the fae to himself kill her?

Lucasian's brow furrowed. "That is the plan, is it not? For you to return me to my full power and finish the last days of your bargain, hopefully enjoying your time in Faerie while staying out of trouble?"

She smiled. "I don't know if I can stay out of trouble."

"I have noticed that about you. Never have I known a mortal who could find themselves in such predicaments as those that befall you. It's as if trouble follows you like a dark cloud."

"That's embarrassingly accurate," she said. "Especially considering you haven't known me long."

"Nor particularly well."

Ros pursed her lips. "You've been inside my mind. I can't imagine how you could possibly know me better than that."

"I did not read your thoughts."

"Because you couldn't?"

"Because I chose not to," he said. "It felt like a betrayal, and considering what I was already asking you to do, I couldn't bring myself to cross that line."

Ros sighed, letting go of a worry she'd had since their time in the library but hadn't voiced. The relief that Lucasian hadn't been privy to her innermost thoughts was a palpable solace, easing more worry than she'd realized she was carrying.

After a moment, she managed, "Thank you for that."

He brushed off her thanks and said, "The last thing I want is to view your mind and somehow understand how you draw such strange, violent attention in your direction."

"It's a gift."

"Let's try to avoid that gift for the rest of your stay," he said, finally giving her a small smile.

"I can try, but no promises."

"Once we get to my home, perhaps you'll be able to spend the next few days relaxing and indulging in all the pleasures that Faerie can offer. Believe me when I say there are many."

Ros felt her stomach plummet at the thought. "No, I won't be able to do that. There's too much trouble waiting at home for me to relax. But maybe I can use the time to plan my next move."

"Telisa is a brilliant tactician," Lucasian said. "I'm sure she'd be happy to help you."

She coughed a laugh. "Oh, I doubt that. She's not very fond of me."

"Really? That's surprising. She was always fond of humans."

"Are we talking about the same Telisa? Tall, devastating, has a tendency to whip out knives and threaten to eat people with little provocation?"

Lucasian laughed. "Well, at least *some* things haven't changed."

Ros bit the inside of her cheek, unsure if she should ask the question jostling through her mind. But of course she would, because she was too curious not to. "Are you afraid of what *has* changed?"

He paused, staring off at a spot in the distance. "I've thought about it more times than you can imagine. Maybe that's why I'm not afraid. My imagination of the world is likely far worse than the truth."

"Still, a lot can change in a thousand years. It could be a completely different world out there."

"I hope it is. I want to enter a kinder world than the one I left behind."

It wasn't the answer she'd expected. Part of her still thought of him as the dangerous fae prince, and the Unseelie Court's brief discussion had made him seem like a hard man to be around. She was seeing a person who'd been away from everything and everyone he'd loved for a millennium, whose greatest desire was to return to a better world. There was something beautiful, poetic in that; but looking at Lucasian, there was also something incredibly sad.

She thought about hugging him. Had it been any of her other friends, she would have. But she wasn't sure that's what they were. He wasn't her enemy, she didn't think, but *friend* also seemed too strong a word. Besides, he still didn't have a shirt on and she wasn't sure her fragile human body could handle such an experience.

That realization made her cheeks flush, and she stepped away from him toward the middle of the antechamber. In an attempt to hide the nerves that had taken over, Ros said, "Let's get this thing started. The sooner you're out of my head, the better."

"Of course," he said, following her across the room. "Ready when you are."

She turned to face him. "I'm ready."

They stared at one another for another moment before Lucasian finally said, "So, uh, are you going to do it?"

"Do what?"

"Transfer my power back."

"You're waiting for me?" she asked. "I don't know how to do that."

"Well, I can't do it. You're the one who absorbed me, so you need to reverse it. Just do the opposite of what you did at the Night Cradle."

"I was dying."

"Well, I'd like to not have to kill you to get this to work."

"Yeah, I'd prefer that as well."

Lucasian rubbed his fingers over his eyes. "I only know what happened from the Night Cradle forward. So, what happened right before you arrived there?"

"My mother poisoned me."

Lucasian said, "That's terrible. Not completely out of

normal bounds though, as you are highly annoying. Sounds a bit like my mother, if I'm being honest."

"She wasn't acting on her own. She was, I don't know, possessed? You've seen her, even if you didn't realize who she was. You saved me from her when we were fighting and she buried me."

"That body was your mother? You know it wasn't *really* her, right?"

"I know something was controlling her."

"Not some*thing*, but some*one*. You were fighting Gaius."

Ros frowned. She wasn't sure she'd ever used his name, at least not since Lucasian entered her mind. She'd always just thought of him as "the darkness."

"How do you know about him?"

Lucasian's face took on a haunted expression before saying, "He tried to set me free."

Eighteen

Rosalinde jerked back as if Lucasian had smacked her. Her head was spinning with the shock of what he'd said, leaving her staring at him slack-jawed and unable to respond.

"What's wrong?" he asked, brows furrowing.

"You..." she stammered. "You're what happened to him? You're the reason he... I don't even *know* what happened exactly. Died? Lost himself to the darkness?"

His eyes widened, and he exclaimed, "No, of course not."

"But you said..."

She trailed off, trying to remember everything Cassian's mother had told them. Ombretta had said that Gaius was dead and that all that remained was the manifestation of his anger. She had said the Night Cradle had killed him when he tried to absorb its power. But it wasn't the Cradle he was trying to control—it was Lucasian. The *Tuath Dé* had killed Gaius and left the foul darkness in his place.

"You killed him."

Lucasian raised his hands. "I think there's been a misunderstanding."

"You tried to use him to escape, but he became that *thing*. He's tormented my family, turned us against one another, destroyed my kingdom. Who knows what else he's done, or what else he's capable of? And it's all because of you."

"You don't understand."

"Is that what's going to happen to me? Are you going to leave a shadow in my stead?"

"Stop," he boomed.

The sound echoed through the tomb, shaking Ros to her core. All her rage died in an instant, replaced by fear. What was she doing? He was an immensely powerful being who could break her any time he wanted. Challenging him was a mistake; her only hope of living through this was to escape. Ros took a deep breath and steadied herself. She could handle anything as long as she faced it head-on and knew what she was dealing with.

And she did.

Lucasian was pure fury, unadulterated rage, a violent creature who could destroy her with a thought. He was...

"Please," he said, his voice cracking.

Ros looked up at him, surprised by the dejection on his face. He was so, so sad.

She had expected anger, and she had steeled herself to deal with that, despite her fear; she hadn't expected sorrow, and certainly not the repentance sitting heavy on his brow. Ros knew nothing of this man before her.

"Gaius could hear me," Lucasian said, his voice cracking. "He could stand in the Cradle and hear me. You do not know what it's like to live on your own for a thousand years and then suddenly someone is there, easing the loneliness. It was a balm I never expected."

She sighed, trying to understand. "So, what happened?"

"We talked. A lot. I'd forgotten how good it could feel to just *talk* to another living being, to someone other than myself. Gaius was clever and inquisitive; at first I thought he must be fae, at least in part, because his mind seemed to work in much the same way as ours. He would ask me questions and make deductions, working to discover who he was, who I was, and how the surrounding worlds interacted. He was interested in power—both how to get it and how to keep it. Sometimes he would remind me of Strahn, and I would try to distance our conversation from the topic of magic, but Gaius would always return to it.

"This went on for years. He was a child, as you would call him, when we met; to me, you are all but babes, death taking you long before maturity evolves you." Lucasian paused for a moment, seeming to take in the heaviness of his own words. With a sigh he continued, saying, "Eventually, years after we'd become friends, Gaius decided he wanted to get me out of here. He'd been reading and researching, but he had no clue what he was doing. I warned him it was a fool's errand. I was trapped eternally, and I'd made my peace with it. He was angry with my response, wanting me to show gratitude or praise his efforts, I'm not sure.

"You have to understand, the interaction I had with him had been an unexpected gift, and I was grateful for his friendship. When he stopped coming to visit, I was as lost as I had been during my first days here. He stayed away for months, until I thought I was destined to spend another thousand years alone. When he next returned, I was so relieved for a respite from the loneliness that I was willing to do anything to make him happy. He told me his plan again to get me out, and this time I didn't chastise him. I embraced his strategy, I praised his intellect and inventiveness, I reinforced the areas where I thought I could help. I was terrified he would leave again and not return."

Lucasian looked down at his hands in disgust, turning them over and over as if they had been the very thing that destroyed Gaius.

Ros put her hands in his, drawing his gaze to hers. She whispered, "Then what happened?"

He opened his mouth, but the words didn't come. Tears filled his eyes, gathered on his long lashes, and slipped down his cheeks. "Then? I mourned him."

"I'm sorry," she said.

Lucasian swallowed. "He reached too far, too deep,

trying to break through. The magic binding me was too powerful for him to break; instead, it burned him from the inside out, corrupting the little that was left of him. It gave him the power he'd been asking about for years, but it destroyed everything in him that was good."

"Leaving only the darkness."

Lucasian nodded. "I couldn't do anything to help him. I would've done anything to stop what was happening—I *should* have stopped it. Though I knew it wouldn't work, I didn't know it would do... that."

"It's not your fault," Ros said.

He pulled his hands away from her and turned away, raking his shaking fingers through his thick hair. "Don't try to ease my guilt. I don't deserve it."

"You don't deserve to punish yourself for his actions, either."

"I could have saved him. I could have spared him from what happened, if only I had been brave enough to face my solitude. If I had pushed him away, he wouldn't have ended up as he did; he wouldn't have hurt you."

"You couldn't have stopped him, no matter what you did or didn't do. He was determined to gain power. His own mother told me so. It sounds like he used his friend-ship with you as a means to an end."

"I could have—"

"Stop," she said. "Just stop. Maybe you could have changed the way it happened, but that doesn't mean he wouldn't have done something else in his search for power.

You didn't make him do anything; you were simply trying to find a piece of joy in your lonely world. No one can fault you for that, especially after you've been trapped here alone all this time. You deserve solace and companionship as much as anyone."

"How do you do that?" he asked, turning back toward her. "How do you empathize so fully, forgive so easily? Why are you so ready to trust someone you barely know?"

She shrugged. "Maybe it's because there's still part of you in my head, but I can *feel* you. The pain of solitude, the desperation to communicate with another soul, the hurt and hatred and regret—I feel it all."

Lucasian reached forward and cupped her face. His thumb raked across her cheekbone, wiping away a tear she hadn't known was there. A tear for him.

In that moment, the only thing Ros truly wanted was to make Lucasian whole. She couldn't undo the past, she couldn't mend the brokenness in him, but she could return that tiny part of him that was missing and hope his life would be better from that moment forward.

A tingle ran over her body. She saw Lucasian's eyes widen, but she didn't understand why until he pulled his hand away from her face. Her single tear glowed gold upon his fingertip. He pressed it to the corner of his own eye and a fog of gold passed through one iris, then the other. Seconds later, it was gone.

He laughed, a true, booming, glorious laugh. Then he threw his arms around her waist and picked her up, spinning her around the antechamber until they were both laughing.

"You did it. You beautiful, fragile, annoying girl."

When he put her down, they were no longer in the tomb. Instead, they stood atop a small green-gray hill—a hill she felt like she'd seen a hundred times—and all around them golden flowers burst into bloom.

Nineteen

Whimsy reacted to their sudden appearance first. Rosalinde heard them shouting, though she couldn't make out the words, then she saw them as they darted up the hill toward her in a blur of fur, followed a bit more leisurely by the Unseelie Court

"You're well," Whimsy said, panting, as a sharp smile gleamed from under slightly matted fur.

Ros thought they were talking to Lucasian, their prince, and shifted to the side to allow them to speak with the man they hadn't seen for hundreds of years. But as she moved, so did Whimsy's gaze, and Ros realized Whimsy was talking to her. She blinked in surprise for a few seconds before asking, "Me?"

Whimsy's smile faltered as they seemed to realize their mistake at the same time Ros had. They dropped to a knee in front of Lucasian and said, "Apologies, Prince Lucasian, for my failure to greet you the instant of your return. Welcome home."

"There's no need for apologies, Datura," Lucasian said as he raised his eyes to the siblings cresting the hill. "Or anyone else. You are here at my resurrection; therefore, I shall know you as my friends. No matter what transpired among us previously," he added, shooting a look toward Sulien. "Today is a new beginning."

Ros looked back and forth between the men. She could tell there was a story there, some long-buried secret, but now was not the time to ask. Still, curiosity burned inside her.

Lucasian pulled Whimsy to their feet and wrapped his arms around the Moonchild's midsection. Despite the sheer size of Lucasian—for he was tall and broad and of formidable size compared to Ros—he barely reached Whimsy's shoulders, and his arms couldn't fully fit around the fae creature. He pressed his face into Whimsy's dark fur, sighed, and, for a moment, finally looked at peace.

"What are your commands, my prince?" Telisa asked. She didn't bother to bow or greet him in any way, but went straight to strategizing. "We can have an assault team ready by this afternoon. Many are still loyal to the *Tuath Dé*, despite the multitude of years that have passed."

Lucasian released the Moonchild and turned to the Spirits of the Air. He put his hand on Telisa's shoulder and for the first time, Ros thought she saw something other than anger on the woman's face. It was a reverence she hadn't known Telisa was capable of from their brief inter-actions thus far.

Lucasian spoke with a softness in his tone reserved for delivering bad news. "I will not be needing an assault team, Teli."

"How will you take the kingdom back?" Telisa asked, her expression shifting between confusion and heartbreak.

"I'm not sure I want it back."

They all looked at the prince as if he'd just sprouted a second head. All except Ros. She understood what it was like to lose her kingdom, and could empathize with Lucasian and the droves of feelings that were surely inter-nally buffeting him. Since she'd been ousted, the most pressing of those feelings was a constant wondering if her kingdom would be better without her. If so, was she willing to give up her own power and position for a better Talabrih?

Lucasian seemed to be willing to let his kingdom continue without him, seeing that it had survived a thou-sand years without him at the helm. Or maybe he hadn't processed any of his emotions and was relishing in his new freedom without a care for the kingdom or the people.

Corbry seemed unsure of himself for the first time since Ros had met him. But he put on a smile anyway, and said, "Your Highness, surely you wish to know what has happened to Faerie in your absence."

"There's plenty of time to talk about the state of the kingdom and figure things out," Lucasian said. "Right now, all I want is to go home."

"Right. About that..." Corbry said, running a hand along the back of his neck. "Your home is, uh, occupied."

Lucasian slowly turned to Corbry, his eyes holding no hint of a smile. "By whom?"

"Oh, you know, some ne'er-do-wells. I will happily run ahead and vanquish them for you, my liege."

Lucasian pursed his lips. "How long have you been living in my house?"

Corbry gave an embarrassed half-chuckle. "Well, I suppose it was around nine-hundred years ago that I realized the *Tuath Dé* homes were empty and needed caretakers. Of course, I eagerly volunteered, wanting to be of service."

"Nine-hundred years," he repeated, his voice barely more than a whisper. He shook his head and said, "After such a time, it surely belongs to you." Lucasian heaved a deep sigh before saying, "Lord Corbry, if it would not be an inconvenience, might I stay in an unused room of your home until I can make alternate arrangements?"

Corbry's eyes widened, making it clear this was not what he had expected. "Yes, of course."

"Thank you," Lucasian said.

Ros was surprised by the man before her. Though she barely knew him, she hadn't expected him to seem so casual once he was freed. Perhaps it was their conversation about Gaius that still had him down, or maybe he was realizing how incredibly different things were going to be from here on out. Either way, he wasn't the conquering hero she'd expected. He was surprisingly timid.

"Would you care to travel by wind, my prince?" Sulien asked.

"No, thank you. I've just realized there are a few things I must do before I return home."

"How can we help?" Telisa asked.

"By caring for my guest," Lucasian said, taking one of Rosalinde's hands in his own.

Ros felt a tingle of magic rush up her arm at his touch. Her breath caught in her chest as her gaze met his. There was a connection between them, their magics recognizing and responding to one another.

"Surely she will return to her own world now that her task is done," Telisa said, barely fighting away the sneer that crept onto her face.

"Her task isn't done," Whimsy said, tilting their head. "Her bond to me is still in place."

"And her bargain with me required ten days."

"That's five more days of quality time we'll have together," Ros said, putting on a bright smile when she caught Telisa's attention.

Corbry's grin grew wide. "What luck! I still have time to convince you to stay in Faerie as Teli's paramour. She's obviously too shy to ask you herself."

"How dare you even suggest—"

"Anyone should feel honored to have family, friend, or lover as strong and clever as our dear human," Lucasian cut in. "After all, it was she who could rescue me from my entombment, and I'm certain you've all tried and failed more times than we could count."

"Absolutely," Corbry said. "Dozens—nay, hundreds of times."

A smile tugged at Lucasian's lips and he said, "As I thought. But Rosalinde figured out a way, and for that, I'm forever grateful."

"Rosalinde, you say?" Corbry's brows rose.

Lucasian winced and looked down at Ros. "You hadn't told them your name?"

"We didn't exactly start on the best footing," Sulien said.

"Just Ros, please," she said. "We're all friends here, after all."

Lucasian nodded. "And I think I would like to be Luc from now on."

"But you always hated it before," Sulien chuckled.

Another look passed between the men, leaving both with rosy cheeks. *Definitely a story,* Ros thought.

With a small smile and a sigh that spoke of a fond memory, Luc said, "I'm off to handle my affairs. It shall only take a faerie's minute."

"A faerie's minute?" Ros asked. "Does that mean it could take a hundred years?"

Luc smiled. "You catch on, don't you?" He turned to Sulien and said, "Take care of my dear friend Ros and do not let her out of your sight. We have five days of keeping her safe. With the likes of us, it should be easy."

Luc snapped his fingers and disappeared. Ros looked around at those left, seeing his last words flashing through her mind. With the likes of these fae, she wasn't sure *anything* would be easy.

Twenty

Ros wiped her mouth after another rough landing from traveling with the Spirits of the Air. She'd been with Corbry this time, and as he laughed heartily at her expense, she knew his abrupt stop was intentional. They were on a tree-lined path paved with coin-sized tiles in shades of orange and red, so that as the sun beat down upon the walk, it looked like they were traveling down a trail of fire.

The path led to the base of a bright green hill bathed in afternoon light. Meadows of wildflowers colored the surrounding valley in turquoise, salmon, violet, periwinkle, canary yellow, and coral.

Perched upon the hill was a home unlike any she'd seen before. Ros had viewed opulence in many forms, many times. Growing up a royal, she'd spent her entire life in elaborate homes for grand events in the presence of the kingdom's nobles. Her own home was a castle dripping with finery. None compared to Lucasian's—now Corbry's —home.

She wasn't sure what the outside was made of, but it wasn't the stone or brick or wood of the homes she'd seen before. It wasn't even as normal as the strange spires of Air house. No, Lucasian's home looked like it was made from obsidian, sliced thin and stacked high upon itself to create a massive glass structure. It seemed both fragile and inde-structible at the same time. The top of the structure was jagged and uneven, but somehow it seemed intentional rather than just unfinished.

"Would you like to see a trick?" Corbry asked.

Ros frowned. Anything coming from Corbry was automatically a trick.

He flashed her a wicked grin. "It won't hurt anyone or anything, including you. No bargains required. Deal?" She pursed her lips and he let out a raucous laugh. "Kidding."

"No deals, no bargains, no tricks."

"I can't win with you," he said, shaking his head as they walked toward the house. "I'm going to show you, anyway."

He waved a hand lazily in front of him, and a wind picked up from the east. It twisted the flowers and grass, then blew through the trees along the path, before finally making its way to the glass castle. The wind twisted through the layers of obsidian and the jagged-edged top of the building, and began to sing.

It was the same song she'd heard Lucasian singing when she awoke that morning. He had been singing the song of his home. The sound was mournful, as if a hundred voices lamented whatever had been lost to them. She understood their sadness; she'd felt it earlier when he sang, the loneliness in him, the ache for lost time. But she felt it in her own heart as well. The voices cried for her lost family and friends, for the love that had been taken from her, for the kingdom she longed to serve.

The song stopped abruptly. "Forgive me, Rosalinde. I didn't intend to upset you. I thought you would like it."

"I do," she said.

"You're crying."

"I've been doing that a lot lately," she said. "But that's fine. Sometimes beauty and pain are synonymous."

If he understood what she meant, he didn't say. Nor did he press to find out what caused her tears. They simply walked up the hill in companionable quiet and stood by the blooming fruit trees in the front yard until the others arrived a few moments later.

When Whimsy joined them, they looked ruffled. "Have I mentioned that I hate traveling by wind?"

Corbry laughed. "Once or twice."

"What happened?" Ros asked.

Whimsy growled. "Nothing worth mentioning."

Sulien and Telisa were there now, both looking sheepish. Telisa asked, "Did you tell them?"

"No," Whimsy said. "Can we just go inside?"

Corbry opened the door and let Whimsy and Ros pass ahead of him. When Telisa and Sulien entered, Ros heard Telisa whisper, "We dropped them."

"They're just so damned heavy," Sulien added.

As they walked through the hall, golden orbs above came to life. They weren't candles or torches like in Water house, but strange balls that seemed to float through the air of their own accord.

"Pixies," Corbry said as he leaned toward her.

"That's horrible."

"Why?"

"You make them work for you, trapped in those globes?"

"Stars no! What would make you think such a thing?" he asked, horror-stricken. "They live here. I give them food and shelter. In return, they light my home. But they're not prisoners. They stay because they're happy and it's safer than the outside world. And the globes are things they made themselves. I'm not entirely sure what they're for."

"Oh, sorry," she said, heat burning up her neck. Yet again she'd applied her human sensibilities to something in Faerie and yet again, she'd been wrong about it.

"Is there somewhere we could rest?" Whimsy asked. "I feel like I haven't stopped moving for..."

They'd just opened one of the many doors along the main corridor and stopped, mouth ajar. Corbry jumped in front of the door and pulled it closed.

"What did I just see?"

"Hard to say," Corbry said, letting out a nervous laugh. "Let's find you some rooms far, far away from here."

Ros smiled and asked, "What are you hiding?"

She reached for the door handle but Whimsy's paw

shot out to her hand and said, "Please trust me when I say that you do not want to see what I just saw."

"Is it bad?" she asked.

"No, not *bad*," Corbry said. "I just left some friends here last night before I went out to dinner with my family. They've likely found something entirely exciting and deliciously debaucherous to do in my absence."

Telisa opened the door a crack and peeked inside. "There's quite a few of them, brother, and it looks like they've started—or continued—without you."

"Yeah, well, I'll get rid of them before Lucasian gets back."

On tiptoes, Sulien leaned over Telisa to look through the door. "You might have a difficult time interrupting some of their... activities."

"I'll just send you in. Nothing ruins a good time faster than my big brother."

"Funny," Sulien said. He pulled back from the door and motioned for Whimsy and Ros to follow him. "Come with me, please. I'll show you to some empty rooms."

"You might need to check and make sure they're empty," Corbry yelled after them. "I'm going to handle this situation, and it might take some intense persuasion on my part, so, uh, don't come looking for me."

THE ROOM where Sulien left her was decorated in black and white. Despite the simplicity of the color scheme, the room was posh; soft blankets and duvets littered the massive, plush canopy bed, the floor was covered in jet-black carpets that her feet practically melted into when she took off her boots, and in the room's corner stood a massive white bathtub.

Ros nearly fainted at the thought of a hot bath. It felt like it had been ages since she'd had such a simple comfort. She tossed her cloak on the floor by her boots and admired the tub. She put her hand against the porcelain and called for her Water magic.

Nothing happened.

"Again?" she asked.

She'd had trouble accessing her magic after leaving Air house, but she thought that was because of the magic poisoning they had used. Since she'd been in Faerie, she hadn't really had a need for her magic with everything else going on, so she hadn't tried to use it. She hoped she was still just getting over the effects of being poisoned, but she feared it was something else.

She couldn't dwell on it, though. There was a bathtub that needed water and a body that needed soaking. Ros crossed the room and stuck her head into the hall. There was no one in sight. She wanted to ask where she could find some water; Ros didn't mind getting it herself, if someone would direct her.

Ros wandered barefoot down the hall. Perhaps she could find Whimsy or Sulien. The floors here were made of marble, like Lucasian's tomb. Hopefully, it wouldn't make him think of that awful place when he walked along this floor like he had walked the antechamber so many times.

She turned a corner into another corridor. This one had a deep purple carpet lining the center of the hall, presumably to keep visitors from getting too close to the art that graced the walls. There were paintings everywhere; mostly they were landscapes and still-lifes, but there were also portraits mixed in here and there. One appeared to be a young Lucasian; she wasn't sure how the *Tuath Dé* aged, and she wondered how long ago it had been painted to capture such a youthful, carefree face.

Farther down the hall, she stopped before another painting bearing his likeness, only he wasn't alone in this one. Three other men and a woman joined him on the canvas. Ros thought they must be his family, though there was little resemblance between them aside from their violet eyes. Lucasian looked down from the painting with his tan skin and honey-gold hair, while next to him stood a man as pale as moonlight, as rigid as marble and seemingly cut from the same, with a swoop of blue-black hair. His eyes were darker than Lucasian's, but there was still a glint of violet in them.

The third man Ros looked at was just as different as the first two. This brother had dark skin and dark hair shaved short. He was shorter than Lucasian and the other man, but still stood tall by human standards. His violet eyes shone brightly from hooded lids, and Ros got a mysterious, yet mischievous impression from him. The final brother was dressed as if he was going to war, a short sword strapped to his hip and the hilt of a larger blade peeking above his shoulder, clearly slung across his back. His thick brown hair was tied back from his face, which was handsome, but still held a youthfulness to it that made him more endearing than intimidating.

Roslainde's eyes at last turned to the woman seated in front of them. A chill ran up her spine. She *knew* her. Younger, yes, but there was no doubt in Rosalinde's head that it was the same woman. How could she possibly be there, in a painting well over a thousand years old, surrounded by fae?

Ros leaned in closer, staring into the much darker eyes of the woman. They weren't the same as the others... but yes, there it was, now that she looked. Eyes that she had taken for black were in actually the darkest shade of violet Ros had ever seen.

"Ah, there you are. I wanted to give you something before I complete my tasks."

Ros jolted at Lucasian's voice. She turned toward him, and before he could say another word, she asked, "Who is this?"

"My brothers," he began.

"Not them. I don't care about them."

"Well that's a bit rude," he said with a chuckle.

"Who is the woman?"

"Are you well?" he asked, brows furrowing. "You're acting very unlike yourself."

"Luc, please."

"It's my little sister," he said. "Her name is—"

"Ombretta," they said in unison.

They stared at one another for a moment before he asked, "How did you know that?"

"Because I know her, I've met her. I'm in love with her son."

"That's impossible," he said, shaking his head. "She's locked away, like the others."

"No, she's not. She's in my world with her two sons. Cassian, the man I hope to marry," she said. Ros paused, looked up into his eyes, and said, "And her eldest son, Gaius. The one who reached out to you; the one who became the darkness."

Twenty-One

Ros sat at a small, plain table in a cramped room adjoining the kitchen. She nibbled on a heel of bread slathered with creamy white cheese that Corbry had raved about the night before. It was fine, not nearly as good as he'd made it out to be, but then again everything seemed to have a sawdust quality to it since she'd had her strange conversation with Luc about his little sister.

It had been a long evening, full of questions she couldn't quite answer about a woman she didn't really know. Luc had been both relieved and furious at the thought of his little sister hiding away in another world while the rest of their family was imprisoned. He understood why she ran, he was grateful she was safe, but he could not grasp why she had never returned to save the brothers she had once so desperately loved.

Ros hadn't seen him yet that morning. He'd disappeared at some point between their evening meal and when she'd finally been able to have a bath, and no one seemed to know where he'd gone. She hoped he was staying out of trouble, just as she'd promised to do, but she had a feeling that trouble followed him the same way it did her.

A circular window above the table slanted up toward the brightening sky, rather than looking out into the garden or over the vineyard she'd discovered behind the house. Above, it was a glorious shade of blue today with not a cloud in her view. The sickness that had affected her when she'd crossed between worlds must have been wearing off, because today was the first day the colors around her hadn't felt too sharp for her eyes. She still occasionally saw blurred colors just outside her field of vision, but perhaps that was just part of Faerie. There always seemed to be something just at the edge of her understanding.

A cabinet banged closed in the kitchen and she flinched. Corbry stood there with a thin red robe draped over him, barely cinched at the waist, and leaving little to the imagination. His hair was pulled up in a sloppy knot on his head, revealing a long neck covered in rows of silver glyphs. The designs trailed to his collarbone and down his chest, continuing lower until she, thankfully, lost them in the folds of his covering.

"Like what you see?"

Ros whipped her attention back to her food, heat rushing to her cheeks. "Your tattoos. I, uh, hadn't noticed them before."

"Because I was wearing clothes," he said. He flipped a chair around on the other side of the table so that when he sat, his arms rested on the back of it. "I could wear less, if it would make your stay in Faerie more... entertaining."

Because of how he sat, Ros knew the only thing between them was the table. Now that he was sitting with, presumably, everything out in the open, she was eternally grateful for that small slab of wood and whoever had placed it in this kitchen so many years ago. Though she still felt the heat in her face from Corbry catching her looking at his exposed body, his flirtations did little to pique her interest. In fact, she only *barely* wanted to lean over the table to see what was under his robe.

"No, thanks. I'm fine without your hospitality."

"Are you certain? I can be quite gracious." He licked his lips.

Ros rolled her eyes. "I'd prefer it if you weren't."

He smiled at her, saying, "You're lucky I haven't used my full charms on you. That nibble of bread couldn't save you. You'd be begging for a private show."

"I highly doubt that."

"Oh, you don't believe I have the charm necessary, or you think your willpower is that strong?"

"I don't think I need willpower to resist your charms."

As soon as the words left her lips, she felt the room shrink around her until there was barely space between the two of them. The room grew so hot Ros felt her skin prickling as if sunburned, accompanied by a pleasant tingling feeling that erupted goose pimples down her body, and suddenly her breast was heaving. She tried to be indifferent when she asked, "What are you doing?" But her own voice turned against her and she heard it as a purr, almost begging him to be *doing* something.

Corbry leaned toward her and took a bite of her bread. He licked the creamy cheese from his lips—something Ros would've been delighted to do for him in that moment—and asked, "What should I take a bite of next?"

Ros swept her arm across the table, knocking everything to the floor. She couldn't seem to stop herself from climbing on top of it to crawl toward him, crossing the distance in an instant. She'd been so grateful only a moment before, but now all she wanted was to remove anything that stopped their bodies from being entwined.

"Stop that," Telisa said, coming up behind Corbry and smacking his head.

For a second longer, Ros *hated* Telisa. She raged inwardly at the woman for ruining this perfect moment that was made just for her and Corbry. Telisa was jealous—it was obvious. But she wouldn't stop their love, wouldn't break the beautiful heat blooming between them...

The room suddenly resolved to what it had been before. The pressure that had surrounded her, the intense need and compulsion to be with Corbry was gone. Ros blinked repeatedly and shook her head, removing the last of Corbry's magic from her thoughts. She climbed off the table, every part of her burning with shame. And anger.

Ros took her seat once again and clenched her hands on the table's edge until her knuckles were white.

"Ow," Corbry said, rubbing the back of his head.

"That was uncalled for," Telisa said, lips pursed.

"I was only making a point. You know I like all participants to be consenting."

Ros finally felt as if she was in control of herself again. She breathed, "What the hell did you do?"

"Turned up the charm," he smirked.

"We all have an ability," Telisa said. "Corbry is the diplomat. He can charm the pants off anyone."

"And I have."

Telisa rolled her eyes. "I'm a strategist. I see things no one else does."

"Not nearly as fun," Corbry said, picking up Rosalinde's breakfast and finishing it in one bite.

"And Sulien—"

"He bores people...to *death*," Corbry finished.

"He's the negotiator," Telisa finished. "Though there hasn't been a need for him for quite a while. I think that's why he's so happy to have Lucasian back."

Ros wasn't sure why Telisa was in such a talkative mood, but she would not miss the opportunity to get some information from her, even if it meant she'd have to hold off on scolding Corbry appropriately. "What's the story with those two? Ex-lovers?"

Telisa and Corbry shared a look. Ros couldn't tell exactly what they were communicating, but she could tell it involved not telling her the history of their brother and the Prince of Shadows.

"Not that," Telisa said. "Definitely not that."

"Rivals, actually," Corbry said. Telisa smacked his shoulder, and he added, "But not really rivals either. I don't know. Let's not talk about this."

"They were both in love with the same person," Whimsy said.

Ros wasn't sure how long they'd been standing there, but clearly it was long enough to know what they were talking about.

"She doesn't need to know," Telisa said.

Whimsy shrugged. "She's leaving in four days. What could it hurt?"

"Do as you will, but I won't be part of it." Telisa huffed and left the kitchen.

As soon as she was gone, Corbry waved Whimsy over and said, "From what I understand, there was a huge falling out between the three of them, though Sulien would never fully commit to telling us the whole truth."

"So, who was this mystery person they were both in love with?" Ros asked, leaning forward on the table.

"I thought you knew," Whimsy said. "Luc said he'd told you how he was entombed."

"He said his friend, Strahn, betrayed him and convinced the Courts to turn on him. But he didn't tell me it was because of a spurned lover."

"Ros, Lucasian *was* the spurned lover. He was in love with Strahn."

"As was Sulien," Corbry said. "When Strahn moved against the *Tuath Dé*, Sulien sided with him to prove his loyalty. He convinced us all to go along with Strahn. Once

Strahn had taken the throne and consolidated all the power for himself, he thanked Sulien for his service and sent him on his way, wanting nothing more to do with him. It took years for Sul to get over that one."

"I... I had no idea."

Corbry nodded. "When I realized which fae prince was being released, I was a little hesitant, to say the least. But I trust my brother, and he believed releasing Luc was the right choice."

"Anything is better than what we've endured," Whimsy muttered.

Ros looked between them. "Is Strahn bad? I mean, obviously he's not great since he locked up all the *Tuath Dé,* but is he bad for Faerie?"

"Are you sure you want to know this?" Corbry asked. "Wouldn't it be better to go home thinking you left Faerie in expert hands?"

"Not if there's something I can do to help."

"There's not," Whimsy said.

"So, he is a poor leader."

"He's... not good," Corbry said. "But Whimsy is right. There's nothing you can do."

"You've already given us the greatest weapon we've had in a thousand years. One of the *Tuath Dé* has returned, and as soon as he figures out how to release his brothers, the land of Faerie will return to its rightful heirs and we can begin to heal."

"He can't release them?" Ros asked. "I thought all you needed was another *Tuath Dé* to get them out."

"So did we," Corbry muttered.

"Prince Luc hasn't figured it out yet, but he will," Whimsy said. His tone sounded confident, but his expression was far less so. "It's nothing for you to worry about."

She wanted to believe Whimsy was right, but her gut told her there was more for her to do yet. Maybe it was what had her tied to Whimsy, tied to this world. She knew what it meant to exist in a kingdom in turmoil, even if she'd only recently realized that's what Talabrih was. So, she would do everything in her power to help these tentative new friends and the kingdom of Faerie. She just had to figure out what exactly she was meant to do.

Twenty-Two

L ater in the afternoon, Corbry invited Rosalinde to go to a local market with him. Though she was still peeved with him for what he'd done to her earlier, Ros wanted to go. The thought of getting out of the house and exploring a bit was exciting, and something she would only have one chance to do. Still, she thought she should consult Whimsy first.

"You want to ask *permission*?" Corbry asked, his face contorted in disgust.

"I want to ask for guidance," she said.

"Because you don't trust me."

"It isn't a matter of trust," she said, "though you're right, I don't trust you. It isn't as if you've given me a reason to put my faith in you."

Corbry pouted his lips. "Fine. I withdraw my invitation."

"No, please don't. I really would love to go."

"I knew it," Corbry said, his pout shifting to a bright smile. "I'll speak with Whimsy on your behalf. I can be incredibly persuasive."

Ros followed Corbry to the study where Whimsy was reading. At a signal from Corbry, she stopped just outside the door and listened as Corbry did his damnedest to win Whimsy to their side.

"Not a chance," Whimsy said, immediately rejecting the idea.

"Datura—"

"No," Whimsy cut in.

"You can trust me."

"We both know I can't."

Ros felt a rush of chilly wind swoop by her. She peeked around the doorway in time to see the curtains in the room swirling violently, as if in a gale. When Corbry spoke, it was not with the casually flirty tone Ros had grown accustomed to over the last few days. There was a gravitas about him that she hadn't expected. He said, "As child of the Northern Wind and Warden of the Eastern Lands, I give my solemn oath to look after Ros and protect her with my life if need be. I grant this promise to you Moonchild, who lives by the name of Datura Whimsy, and voluntarily place myself in your service until such a time as I return the mortal safely to your care."

There was a long silence between them, but then the winds died down and everything seemed to return to normal. Corbry's oath seemed to ease Whimsy's worry and assure them that Corbry was offering his guarantee as only one of the fae could. Finally, Whimsy said, "I accept your promise."

Once Whimsy had agreed, Corbry's air of nonchalance immediately returned. "I can't imagine why that was necessary. It's just the local market, after all. In a place such as that, who would be stronger than me if it came down to a fight?"

"Why would it come to a fight?" Whimsy asked.

Corbry laughed. "I'm just making a statement, friend. Don't be so literal."

A low, frustrated growl shook from Whimsy's throat. "Words have power. Speak what you mean, and nothing more."

Corbry sighed and waved a dismissive hand. "We'll only be around weaker fae for the hour or so we'll be gone. I can protect our little darling for at least that long."

"Fine, but before you go, I have something for Ros." Their voice louder, Whimsy said, "I know you're there, human. You can come out."

She stepped around the corner and asked, "How did you know I was there? I was so quiet."

"You think I can't smell a human at twenty paces? Please."

Ros held her hand to her nose. It still smelled of the mint leaves Sulien had given her for her bath the night before. "Do we really have a unique smell?"

"Yes," they both said.

"Is it good or bad?"

"Mostly good," Corbry said. "Though it has a tendency to make me hungry."

"Is that why you're always eating around me?"

"Corbry just likes to eat," Sulien said as he entered the room. "You know, faeries only need to eat once every couple of years to stay alive. We do it more because we enjoy it. But my little brother here eats more than anyone I've ever met, including the mortals with whom I've been acquainted. It's always been a weakness."

"You call it a weakness, but I think it's a pleasure. What more is there to life than great food and good company?"

"Loyalty, love, responsibility..." Sulien ticked off on his fingers.

"Rubbish when compared to a strong cheese and a stout beer."

"Speaking of cheese and beer," Ros cut in, "we're going to the market. Would you like us to bring anything back for you?"

"Which market?"

"Grimsby," Corbry said.

"Can you check with the bookshop to see if my orders are in?"

Corbry rolled his eyes. "Errands are already notoriously boring. I didn't believe you could improve upon that, yet still you managed. Sending me to a bookshop is a particularly cruel punishment, brother mine."

Ros smacked his arm. "I love books, I'll have you know."

"Of course you do."

"Wear a familial cloak, just in case," Sulien said.

He tossed Ros a wad of sapphire that seemed to have appeared from nowhere. She unfurled it to find a beautifully crafted outer cloak lined with fur. She swung it over her shoulders and tied it into place, leaving the hood down. Upon the left breast was the symbol of a triangle with a line through it. Ros had seen the same symbol on Corbry's body that morning.

"What's this?"

"It marks you as a servant of the winds," Corbry said. "None of the lesser fae will bother you once they see it."

"You should wear this, also," Whimsy said. They handed her a delicate gold chain with an oblong jade stone attached by gold filigree. "It's a gift from Prince Luc. He'd planned to give it to you himself, but now may be a splendid opportunity to try it out."

Ros slipped it around her neck. "It's lovely."

"And powerful," Corbry said, brows furrowed. "I can feel it pushing against my power and I'm only barely trying to seduce you."

Sulien sighed heavily and said, "Stop. Trying. To. Seduce. Her."

Ros pursed her lips, finally finding the right moment to address Corbry's previous behavior. "You know, I heard the promise you made to Whimsy. As long as you're handing out solemn vows today, there's one I'd like to have from you."

Corbry raised his brows, surprise and delight warring for control of his face. "Ask it, love."

She knew she was on dangerous ground. The Spirits of the Air were volatile and somewhat fickle, from what she'd seen. Her next words could turn Corbry's good nature against her. She had to say it, though she was asking a lot of him—her request was contrary to his very nature. Ros knew she would never forgive herself if she didn't use what little favor she had gained with him to make things better for the mortals who would come after her. She said, "As long as your life lingers on, you are never again to use your charms on a human."

Corbry swallowed. He took a moment to consider her request before saying, "And what do you offer to entice me to this vow?"

It was Rosalinde's turn to offer something. But what could a fae such as he ask that she could give him? "What will you have of me?"

A wry smile crossed his lips, but in answer he only said, "I will do as you ask, little human."

"At what cost?"

Corbry shook his head. "A gift, with nothing returned. The cost is nil."

"Why would you do that?"

"To show my good nature."

Ros furrowed her brows. "You promise?"

He shrugged. "I'll keep my word, darling. I'll never use my gift on a human again. But I'm obviously going to keep trying by normal means. And, of course, my *normal* means are often enough."

She was beginning to think he couldn't help himself

from making advances, as it was part of his gift, but she refused to give him an excuse, even if his flirtations were mostly harmless.

"Even if he tried to use his charms, this boon of Luc's will protect you against fae control," Whimsy said.

"How does it work?"

They said, "You already know the basic ways of guarding yourself, but there are a handful of incredibly powerful creatures in Faerie who can gain control of humans without food or bowing. You aren't likely to meet anyone stronger than the Spirits of the Air, and certainly no one stronger than Prince Luc."

"What can these other fae do?" she asked.

"Just being in their presence could sway you toward them."

"Like when Corbry uses his charm?"

"So you *do* admit it," Corbry smirked.

"And the persuasion Telisa was using when we first met you at Craicholme," Sulien said. "Whimsy fed you bread to counteract it—smart, by the way—but she could've pressed it further and kept control. The bread was enough to discourage her though, and with Telisa, that's her weakness. If she loses the advantage, she'll switch tactics."

"Luckily, she's on our side now," Whimsy said.

"Mostly," Corbry shrugged.

The Grimsby market was busier than Ros had expected. Corbry had made it sound as if the place would be deserted, but now she realized that had been part of his ploy to get her here. Now that she was here, it was a little overwhelming.

It wasn't as big as Craicholme had been, but there she'd been with Whimsy and had felt protected even when facing down the Unseelie Court. With Corbry as her guardian, it wasn't the same. She knew he wouldn't allow anyone to hurt her if he saw something amiss, but as soon as they'd entered the market, Corbry had almost entirely forgotten her presence as he became engrossed in the vendors and their wares, leaving her to wander behind him carrying baskets of the things he bought. Her big blue cloak was truly suiting her in that moment, as she felt like a servant of their house.

They were perusing a textile stall now, where colorful cloth hung in ribbons and swathes from the ceiling, and bolts of fabric leaned haphazardly against every surface. She closed her eyes for a moment, breathing in the smoky aroma of charred meats wafting over from another stall.

"Those are lovely blood pears you have there."

Rosalinde's eyes jerked open and she turned to the voice, surprised to see a man who looked remarkably human, while still undeniably fae. He was tall and fair, handsome in a strange, pointed way. His features were sharp, almost jagged, as if his very touch would cut her. Looking at him made her feel that same "too muchness" she had felt when she'd first arrived in Faerie. He had hair of spun gold and eyes...

Oh no, she thought. *Eyes like the morning tide.*

Whimsy had told her to run, RUN, if she ever saw a man like that. But how could she? He was there, looking at her, talking to her, and Corbry—

She looked around, but Corbry was nowhere to be seen.

"Yes," Ros replied, swallowing against the lump rising in her throat. She felt the filigree chain growing heavy around her neck; despite the lightness of it, the thin filigree now seemed to weigh more than she did. But it was there, weighing her down, yes, but protecting her. She found her voice again, and somehow her diplomatic training jolted into place with a smile. "They look delicious, don't they?"

The man licked his lips. Ros got the distinct impression it wasn't the blood pears he was hungry for.

"Forgive me for being so forward, but you are human, aren't you?"

Ros felt a writhing in her gut. He knew the answer to his question already. There was no point trying to lie to one of the high Fae, and surely he was one of them. Still, everything within her begged that she not say it aloud. She didn't want to admit it, to expose the weakness so clearly visible to one such as he. But she had to.

She choked down her fear and said, "I am."

He smiled so brightly at her words, the rest of the world seemed to dim in comparison. "I thought so. It's been far too long since I've had the pleasure of a mortal's company. Would you like to take a walk with me?"

Ros felt the magic in his words as it washed over her and her feet took a step toward him of their own accord. Even with Lucasian's charm shielding her, she felt her will within her tugged to bend toward this man's will. Had Whimsy not delivered the trinket earlier than Luc meant for it, she would be utterly powerless against him.

Forcing her lips to part and her voice to ease out, she managed to whisper, "A kind offer, good sir, but I have prior engagements."

He tilted his head, a tiny crease forming between his brows. "You are denying my request?"

She looked up into his eyes—so blue nothing else could ever be described as that color—and said, "Regrettable, but I must."

Without warning, he reached forward and cupped his hand to her cheek. "So much *life* flowing through you, mortal girl. Your skin is as red and juicy as the fruit in your basket. It makes me want to just eat you up."

The only thing keeping Ros from running as fast as she could away from this creature was the knowledge that it would only make a more enjoyable sport for him. Instead, she planted her feet, fighting every fiber of her being as it begged her to do his bidding, and she willed her voice to remain steady. Conjuring every portion of her royal demeanor that she could, every minute of training through the years where her mother had instructed her on composure or her father had guided her on having an *aura* of power, Ros said, "Remove your hand from me."

He held firm a second longer before releasing her. His expression changed from hungry to confused. He looked at his own hand as if it had betrayed him. Swallowing hard, he said, "Forgive me, young one. I have behaved regrettably."

He took a step back from her, shaking his head. Every movement he made as he removed himself from her presence seemed to change him slightly. His golden hair lost its luster, no longer appearing as spun gold. His eyes faded from polished lapis lazuli to a common human blue. The man was still handsome, the lines of him still sharp like the facets of a diamond, but he was *less* than he had been a moment before. It was as if her refusal of his will had hollowed out the power of his magic.

He glanced at the symbol on her cloak, recognition clear on his face. With a tone that sounded truly affronted by his own actions, he said, "Beg your master's forgiveness of me, and yours. Please."

Before she could take a breath, he was gone. Vanished into the air faster than the Spirits themselves.

Ros could still feel his fingertips upon her cheek.

Twenty-Three

Several minutes later—or longer, she wasn't completely sure—Ros recounted the story to Corbry when he found her shaking in front of a carpet vendor down the row of stalls. He had stepped away to gather Sulien's books, he said, expecting that she wouldn't even notice him gone. Perhaps she wouldn't have had she not encountered the high fae.

"Let's get you home," Corbry said. Ros reached for the baskets at her feet and he said, "Leave them."

He took her hand and they wind-walked to the obsidian castle. Upon arrival, they touched down like a feather floating on the wind, proving that he didn't have to make her landing so rough that she puked; he simply enjoyed it.

Whimsy met them at the door. "What happened?"

"How did you know something happened?" Corbry asked.

The Moonchild lifted Ros into their arms and carried her inside, sitting her down in a plush armchair in the parlor before they answered Corbry. "I felt it. Her fear left a vile taste in the back of my throat."

"How?"

"We're bonded through the words of the *Tuath Dé*, though I still don't know what business we have together. Now please, tell me what happened."

Before Corbry could explain, Sulien rushed into the room. He knelt in front of Ros, and when he spoke, his voice was hard as stone. "Did he hurt you?"

"No," she breathed. "But he wanted to."

"Tell me," Whimsy growled, looking between the brothers.

Sulien handed him a slip of parchment with gold writing upon it. "An apology letter, for frightening my servant. And an invitation to the grand ball at the palace."

"Strahn?" Whimsy asked. Their eyes jerked up to Corbry. "You saw Strahn at the market? You let him talk to her?"

"I didn't," Corbry said.

"It wasn't his fault," Ros said. "He was picking up Sulien's order and—"

"YOU LEFT HER ALONE?" Whimsy boomed.

Ros jerked back in her chair as Whimsy's body seemed to grow taller, broader, and their fur became as dark as midnight, a void from which no color escaped.

Corbry backed away, hands raised, as the Moonchild

prowled toward him. "It was an accident. There was nothing going on in the market, so I thought she'd be fine for a few minutes."

"Calm down," Sulien yelled. "Whimsy, please..."

But Whimsy would not be quelled. An electricity hummed through the air. Ros could feel it in her teeth, a bone-aching shock vibrating through the room. Her hair stood up on end as static consumed the area around her.

The very air entering her lungs began to sting her, to send an ache through her body. She screamed, "What's happening?"

The parlor door burst open and Telisa ran in. In two long strides, she jumped, catching her foot on the edge of the table to propel her high enough to reach Whimsy's elongated shoulders. She got her arms around their neck and climbed up their body like they were a tree. At that moment, they had grown as big as one.

Whimsy swatted at her once, twice, as if she were a gnat. They didn't bother trying to fight her off further, keeping their eyes on the Warden of the Eastern Lands, who had broken his oath to guard Ros from trouble. Whimsy swung out one of their massive paws and back-handed Corbry, flinging him into the wall like a rag doll.

Telisa had managed to get her legs around Whimsy's neck now. She wrapped her arms around their head, covering their eyes so they couldn't see the youngest of the elves, and Sulien grabbed Corbry's prone body and hefted him out of the room.

Whimsy's movements slowed as Telisa squeezed her legs to apply pressure around their neck. As if in half-speed, the Moonchild came to a halt, shrinking back to normal size and falling to the ground at Rosalinde's feet.

Telisa climbed off them, panting and gleaming with sweat. She paused in front of Ros and, without looking at her, asked in a husky voice, "Are you well?"

"Y-yes. But what about them?"

"Whimsy will be fine. They'll wake in a few minutes and won't remember what happened once they grew enraged. Give them water with a heap of sugar in it."

She started out of the room, but Ros called after her, "What about Corbry?"

Telisa paused, one hand on the door. "I don't know. Whimsy was unable to grow to their full power, constrained by the size of the room. If they'd been at full strength, Corbry would be dead. Half strength though? There's a chance he'll be fine. Either way, now he'll know better than to make oaths to mortals and Moonchildren."

She closed the door then, leaving Ros alone with a sleeping Whimsy and a lot of questions.

WHIMSY SIPPED the sugar-water and stared at their hands while Ros told them what had happened. As Telisa had predicted, they remembered nothing after discovering that Corbry had left Ros alone in the market.

"I saw the whole thing with my own eyes, but I still don't understand what happened."

Whimsy grimaced. "I'd prefer if you never knew that side of me."

"It's too late for that now, friend."

They looked up at Rosalinde's words. "Friend?"

Ros shrugged. "Of course. At least, that's how I feel at this point. Is it offensive for a child of Faerie to be friends with a mortal?"

"Offensive? No. But rare. Can you still call me that after seeing what I did?"

"You were upset, and you did something you regret. That doesn't change our friendship."

Whimsy put one of their paws over Rosalinde's hand. "You continue to surprise me, human."

Ros smiled. "You definitely surprised me today, too."

ROS WENT to see Corbry on Whimsy's behalf after Telisa had refused the Moonchild entry. She eased into his room on socked feet, trying to keep from waking him. To her surprise, he was already awake.

"Fancy meeting you here," he said through swollen lips.

"They couldn't keep me away. I guess your charms really do work."

"I knew it." He chuckled, coughed. Putting his hand on his side and wincing, Corbry said, "I've got three busted ribs, a broken collarbone, a fractured wrist, and blurry vision in one eye. But I'm still a stone-cold fox."

"Whimsy wanted to tell you—"

"No," Corbry said, waving his hand. "You tell Whimsy something for me."

Ros nodded, expecting the worst. She swallowed, saying, "Of course."

"Tell them I'm sorry."

"You're... sorry?"

Corbry patted the bed beside him and Ros sat down. He whispered, "I'm so sorry. I invited you to go with me, I gave an oath of protection, but I didn't take care of you. I didn't take it seriously, despite my promise, because Strahn's presence was not something I anticipated. Instead of honoring my word to Whimsy, I dismissed their worry as foolishness because of something I could not foresee. You were in danger while I was off flirting."

"I thought you were getting Sulien's books."

"I was," Corbry said. The corner of his mouth tilted in what would have been a wicked grin if his lips weren't so beat up. "Is it my fault that booksellers find me attractive? No, because they have a pulse, and that's all it takes to desire me."

Ros laughed. "If you weren't already in awful shape, I'd punch you myself."

"I'd probably deserve it. You know, I'm honestly surprised it's taken this long for someone to throw me across the room."

She pressed her lips into a grim line. Ros knew Corbry was keeping up his banter for her sake, so she didn't realize how hurt he really was. "Will you make it through this?"

"Of course," he said. "Once our beloved prince returns, he can heal me right up. Or at least, I hope he will. If he decides to knock some sense into me as well, I'm a goner."

"Where is he, anyway?"

"Unclear. He's been strangely absent for a guy who hasn't had any company for a thousand years. I thought he'd be more clingy."

"Maybe he doesn't know how to deal with people anymore," Ros said.

"Or maybe he's out reacquainting himself with people, if you know what I mean."

"I think I do..."

"Sex," Corbry said.

"Yeah, I get it."

"I would be. Can you imagine going that long without another person touching you?"

"Forget the sex," she said. "He hasn't even had someone to hug, or talk to, or even look at for all that time."

"Right, sure," Corbry said. "But a thousand years without sex. Think about it."

Ros smiled at Corbry's insistence, but he had a point. Lucasian had been alone for a long time; the idea that he might go out to find some company wasn't that strange.

"Whenever you see him, tell him to stop by for a visit,"

Corbry said. "He can heal me, and I'll be so grateful, he won't have to leave the house if he wants some attention."

Ros rolled her eyes and stood up. "You're incorrigible."

"And you love it."

She smiled, and against her better judgment, she said, "I guess I do."

Twenty-Four

~~~

L uc still hadn't returned the next morning when a courier arrived at their door. Ros had gone to answer it, as she still hadn't seen a servant present in the obsidian house, but Telisa pushed her out of the way just as her hand hit the doorknob.

"Stop taking unnecessary risks, human."

Ros stood behind the door while Telisa talked to the messenger. She could see the fae creature through the crack; it was the size of a human child, with glittery seafoam-tinted skin and a shock of white hair. There were vast wings tucked against its back, shining in iridescent colors of amethyst, magenta, and chartreuse.

It wasn't until Telisa closed the door that Ros saw the package in her hands. It was a long gold box with a thick velvet ribbon the shade of blood. "What's that?"

The woman shot her a look. "It's clear that I haven't opened it yet, so why would you ask?"

Ros shrugged. "I thought maybe the faerie told you."

Telisa picked up a card attached to the ribbon and read: "For your servant, as an apology and a guarantee that she will be the most alluring creature at tonight's festivities."

The women locked eyes for a moment. The excitement and curiosity Ros had felt only a moment before had vanished, replaced by a dread she couldn't quite name. Telisa opened the box. She pushed aside gold-flecked tissue paper to reveal a swathe of sapphire the same color as the cloak she'd worn to the market.

Telisa sighed. "Get Sulien. Tell him we're out of excuses. The two of you are going to a ball."

THERE WERE hours of planning and plotting that afternoon, and Ros got the chance to see Telisa in all her glory. She truly was a masterful tactician, and watching her mind calculate and project their gift was strangely beautiful.

When all was said and done, they had a tentative idea of what they were going to do, though none of them were happy about it. Even with Telisa's brilliance, there was too much they couldn't account for. Though the Spirits of the Air had all been to the High Ruler's ballroom before, the venue was the least important aspect of their plan. Based on their assessment, Strahn could have the ball in an open field where anyone could come at him on any side and he would still be nigh impenetrable. The odds were not in their favor.

Still, they prepared.

There were no other options. His invitation was more of a demand than a request. If they did not attend of their own volition, the next fae knocking on their door would be far more dangerous than the creature who had flitted over that afternoon. The siblings were certain they could handle *some* of the fae who Strahn might send, but they had no qualms admitting they were weak against the high Ruler himself. He would find them himself if they chose to show him disrespect, and none were willing to risk facing him in open rebellion.

With choice removed, the Spirits of the Air did the best they could with what they had and set about preparing to attend a ball. As it turned out, Corbry was much better at preparing to attend a ball than he was at planning a contingency for when things inevitably went wrong. He had them looking far better than a human and a perpetually grumpy entity had any right to, and sooner than any of them liked, they were setting off for a troublesome night they'd all prefer to avoid.

They arrived by wind to the home of the most powerful lord in the land: Strahn, the High Ruler of Faerie. Ros wore the dress that had been sent, despite initial protests and multiple verifications that it wasn't spelled. It hugged her curves in a way that both flattered and made her uncomfortable. She'd never been shy about showing her body and encouraged women around her to be comfortable in whatever body they had, but something about this dress made her hyper-aware of the eyes on her.

As she and Sulien entered the ball arm in arm, *every* eye was on her. No matter which direction she looked, she caught the eye of a faerie looking at Strahn's chosen dress.

Sulien sighed a shaky breath and whispered. "Just smile. Breathe. Try to enjoy yourself."

She tried to take his advice, ignoring the eyes on her. It wasn't as if it was the first time people had stared at her, and it wouldn't be the last. She'd received nearly as much attention a little over a month ago when she'd tripped on the stairs and fallen into Cassian's arms. If something good could come from that embarrassment, surely she could find something pleasurable in the enchanting world of the fae.

Ros had been to balls before, but no celebration in the human world could ever compare to the sight before her. Once the faeries lost interest in her and returned to their conversations, she felt better about letting her gaze roam the room, though she was unsure where to look first. When she finally settled her eyes on one thing, something else came along to vie for her attention.

The room itself had an open ceiling, but there was a dome above it created with crisscrossing branches and vines that grew from the massive trees surrounding the palace. She could see hints of starlight through them occasionally, twinkling down to add another layer of enchantment.

Ros marveled at the glowing orbs suspended from the ceiling, giving off a warm, golden light—more pixies. Though she'd seen them at Lucasian's house, they were few in comparison with those swarming through the room above her. The orbs seemed to go where they were needed, giving light to those who wished it and giving privacy to those with salacious intent. She couldn't help but wonder if they were here of their own accord as they were at Lucasian's home, or if these pixies were forced to be here in service to Faerie's lord.

There were tables and chairs set up around the room. Fae creatures of all sizes and shapes perched there, talking and laughing and drinking. Ros watched a fragile-looking fae with iridescent blue wings, similar to the messenger, chug a pint of ale in a matter of seconds; a sprite the size of Rosalinde's hand danced with a humanoid fae whose features were distinctly fishlike; a team of dwarves carved wooden sculptures in the corner of the room, and no one seemed surprised when their creations came to life.

"After what happened yesterday, I'm loath to say this," Sulien said once they were settled into a quiet corner of the room, "but I need to leave you alone for a few minutes."

"What? Why?"

"I just spotted my contact from Strahn's inner circle. I need to find out if there's been any word of Lucasian to reach the Lord Ruler."

"Can't I go with you?"

Sulien shook his head. "It'll be easier for a fae to slip unnoticed through the crowds. A human, especially in a dress like that, will draw too many hungry eyes."

Ros looked down at her dress again. It was strapless, showing an unholy amount of her assets. It curved tightly along her body until it reached mid-thigh, where it finally loosened up before cascading to the floor.

"What if he finds me again? I can't run in this thing."

"He won't hurt you, not in a room full of people, at least. Just stick to the edges of the room and don't touch anything or talk to anyone, if you can help it."

"What if I can't help it? Trouble always finds me."

"Not today," Sulien said. "You're going to blend into the wall and disappear."

"How do I do that?"

Sulien shrugged. "I'm not sure. I do it by accident quite often."

Ros smiled. It was the first time she'd heard Sulien attempt a joke, and the simplicity of it was immensely relaxing.

He gave her a smile in return and said, "You'll be fine. I'll be back in a moment."

She wasn't happy about it, but she gave a nod and watched Sulien slip through the crowd, moving away from her toward a shadowed alcove in the back of the room.

A servant in green livery passed by, offering Ros a plate of food. Her mouth watered just looking at the delicacies and every part of her ached to try a taste of everything, but Whimsy's warnings rang out over and over in her head: *Never eat faerie food. Never eat faerie food. Never eat...*

And this was most certainly "faerie" food. It wasn't like the denock meat and eggs Whimsy had given her on her first morning in a new world, nor was it similar to the tavern food Corbry had ordered, or the wares in the market where she'd met Strahn. Those foods were common, prepared for sustenance, and though those straightforward items were still part of Faerie and made by fae hands, they were vastly different than the towering treats present here.

This food looked decadent. Mounds of chocolate, caramels the size of her fist, fizzy drinks in vibrant magenta and darkened plum, cakes drizzled in honey and secrets, begging to coat her tongue in sugar and sin.

No bread anywhere.

She had a piece of it strapped to her thigh alongside one of Telisa's blades, both of which Whimsy had insisted on despite how difficult they would be to access. She hoped she would not need them.

Ros turned away from the refreshments and turned back to the party, where dancers had taken up a jig she'd never seen before. The movements were intricate and hypnotic to watch. The entire room seemed pulled into the ebb and flow of the movement until there was nothing but the dance.

"Are you enjoying yourself?"

Ros jumped, startled by the deep voice of the man at her side. She stared at him for a moment, searching for horns or wings, anything to mark him as fae.

"I'm human," he said at her wordless inquiry, his lips twitching in a smile.

"Sorry," she said, though she was unsure what made her want to apologize. She stared at him for a moment, enjoying the sight of another human in the midst of Faerie. He was taller than her, though not by much, with olive skin that seemed to shimmer in the light, almost as capti-vating as one of the fae. His eyes were a rich brown, his wide nose perched over lips that begged to be kissed. In another world—her world—she would have been smitten.

"Don't be sorry," he said, wrapping an arm over her shoulder and guiding her around the room. "That's usually the thing that makes me stand out at things like this. I can win the attention of every eye, have my pick of distractions and devilish delights simply by existing in this place that isn't my home."

"And where is your home?"

"A world far from here, in a land called New York. But I've lived here for many years now. Where are you from?"

"My kingdom is called Talabrih."

The man sipped from a fluted glass before saying, "Never heard of it."

Ros smiled, trying to look unbothered. "Do you like it here?"

"Most of the time. The fae can be unpleasant when they're denied their desires, but most of the time they are delightful. The best thing you can do to survive Faerie is to give in to their wills. Give the fae what they want."

"That doesn't sound enjoyable."

The man shrugged. "It is if you let yourself give in to your own desires. You'll often find them interconnected with the fae. Tonight I will let myself be pulled in a dozen directions until I end up with whoever has the strongest desire. Normally this game would be enough to keep the higher fae busy, but it seems I am not the only entertainment for this evening." He looked her up and down, brows raising. "Guess I've got some competition."

It took Ros a moment to realize he was talking about her. She certainly didn't feel like anyone's rival, especially when she could look in any direction and see the most beautiful thing her eyes had ever beheld. The grandeur of it all was intoxicating.

Though she had been the talk of the place when she'd entered, interest in her had waned quickly. She said, "I'm flattered, I assure you, but no one is looking at me when there's so much else to enjoy."

The man pursed his lips. "Lord Strahn hasn't taken his eyes off you since you entered the room. He has all of Faerie at his disposal, but his gaze rests on a human girl. Why is that?"

"He's here?" she asked, looking around.

"And a hopeless girl at that," the man muttered. Before Ros could respond, he walked away, leaving her standing in the middle of the room.

Ros wasn't sure when she'd made her way there; she'd been so caught up in their conversation as she'd walked alongside the man that she hadn't noticed where he led her. Now the dancing had stopped and she was all alone, a ring of vicious glares in every direction she looked, staring from the circle that enclosed her. She gulped back the fear rising in her gut. Her throat was suddenly so dry, she thought she might literally murder someone for a drink...

She looked at her hand and realized there was an empty flute glass in it. Ros didn't remember taking it, didn't remember drinking from it, but there it was, the stem dangling between her fingers.

Bread. She needed to get out of sight to get the slice they'd tied to her thigh. She looked around, searching for an escape, but she was penned in on all sides by the crowd of fae who seemed to now find her as the most interesting part of the ball.

Then her eyes found Strahn. The High Ruler of Faerie stood at the edge of the room, stepping down from a throne carved from a giant, golden apple. Ros hadn't noticed him at first, because so much else had warred for her attention, but now she could look nowhere else.

And she didn't need to, for he was staring right at her. What else in all the worlds was more important than his attention? She could think of nothing worthy to compare him to, no one who rivaled him. Though she hadn't realized it until this very moment, she would do anything for him. He was her everything.

The room grew small until they were the only two people there, staring at one another, moving under one another's gravitational pull. Ros stepped toward him, delighted to see his lips twitch up into a smile at her tentative approach. Her heart beat like a drum, begging her to go to him. She took another step.

A warm hand wrapped around her upper arm, rooting her in place. Ros wanted to turn and see who held her, to jerk her arm from their grip and escape them, but the thought of taking her eyes from Strahn was too painful. She had to get loose, had to get to him as soon as possible or else she might die, her heart exploding from the sheer pain of not being with him.

She bucked against the hand, trying to rip her arm free, but they held firm. She pulled again, desperate to rid herself of whoever was keeping her from her beloved.

A gray-skinned man with silver hair stepped in front of her, cutting off her line of sight to the High Ruler. She looked up into gray-green eyes. They were full of kindness, and something else... alarm, maybe? What plagued his thoughts and worried him so? She couldn't be sure. It didn't matter anyway. He was not Strahn, and Strahn was all that she needed to be well and whole.

"Are you all right, Rosalinde?"

She tilted her head as she stared up into his face. He spoke her name as if he knew her, and maybe he had, in another life. In this life, though, there was only one thing that mattered.

"I need to reach my beloved."

The man put his hand on her shoulders and said, "Oh, darling, the ruler of the kingdom cares for you deeply and has sent me to help you get to him. There is something you must do for him before you will be able to tolerate his presence. He is so strong, his magic so powerful, that few can be near him."

"I've been near him before."

"Yes," the man said, "of course you have. And our great ruler sent me to you because he wishes you to join him again."

"He does?" Ros asked, her face beaming at the thought of Strahn making special arrangements for her.

"Lord Sulien," Strahn called, his voice echoing through the room. "What are you up to?"

The man drew a leather strap from around his neck. There was a small vial tied to it, with tiny tan granules inside. "Yes, of course. Didn't you hear how Lord Strahn called my name to see what I was doing? The Lord of Faerie wants you to have this. Tip it up like a drink, and then you're free to go to him."

Something niggled at the back of her head, a warning of some kind. Was this a bad fae creature trying to harm her? No, Strahn would protect her. None would harm her once she was at his side. And he *had* called out to the creature, after all. If this was a gift sent from the High Ruler and she didn't drink it, would he still want her? Could she be in his presence for eternity if she refused his kindness now? Everything was so confusing.

"Why can't he give it to me?" Ros asked, pushing her way through the clouds of confusion.

"He can't give it to you himself without causing an uproar amongst the Court. They will all be so jealous of his attention that you would be unsafe. But he promised everything would be clear to you once you drink it, and you will be out of harm's way. Doesn't that sound nice?"

It did sound nice. She wanted to understand what was going on, not only for herself, but for her love. Ros took the vial from the fae's hand, popped the cork, and tipped it back in one quick gulp.

"Enough of this," Strahn said. "You'll not weave your way out of this spell, wordsmith. Not when I already have this."

The man stepped aside and Ros could see Lord Strahn again. The High Fae held up his hand, where a jade gemstone dangled from a chain.

Rosalinde's hand shot to her chest. It was her necklace, the one Lucasian had given her to keep her safe from fae tricks. *Lucasian.* He was her friend, wasn't he? And an enemy of the man who now held her necklace. Her love. *No, that wasn't right.* How did he get her charm? And why did he want it? She was just an insignificant human in a world where everything and everyone was rare and beautiful.

Then she noticed the handsome human man at Strahn's side, the man from New York. The sneaky little... Her head throbbed suddenly with a fierceness that doubled her over.

"Come to me," Strahn said.

Ros felt her body lurch toward him of its own accord. She wasn't the only one; throughout the room, nearly everyone took a step toward him, his voice digging into the bones of all who heard it.

She grabbed Sulien's arm. *Sulien.* Of course. She knew him now. How had she not recognized him before? And he had given her bread. A tiny bit he had smuggled in, but it had helped her combat the spell she'd been under. She knew it wasn't enough to fight Strahn for long; they had warned her that the High Fae could use magic far stronger than her bread and necklace could fight. Those things were merely meant to help her last long enough to get away. Where could she run from the highest faerie in the land?

Strahn stepped down into the crowd and moved toward her. Faeries parted for him, none wanting to deter him from getting what he wanted. None were willing to incur his wrath.

Except Sulien. He stepped between them wordlessly, using his arms to shield her.

"Out of the way, Sulien. I want a look at the pet you've brought me."

Sulien shook his head. "I'm sorry, my lord, but I cannot do that. My house has grown attached to this girl and we do not wish to offer her to you."

There was a gasp from the watching crowd. Even Strahn wore a look of surprise. "Excuse me, but are you telling me I can't have what I desire?"

Rosalinde watched Sulien's shoulders square in front of her, his body tense as he faced down the High Ruler of Faerie. He said, "That's exactly what I'm telling you."

"Well, well, it seems our mild-mannered Sulien has finally grown a backbone. It only took a thousand years."

Several people in the crowd laughed, and Ros could see the muscles in Sulien's neck flex. Whoever he had been before was not the same as who he was now. He would stand up for Lucasian, stand up for her, and protect the things he needed to protect.

"I—"

Strahn whipped two fingers through the air. A spray of

red flecked his cheeks as his lips curled in a smile. "I can't have that."

Ros ran in front of Sulien and dropped to her knees at the same time he did. His hands were raised to cover the gash in his neck, but blood rushed out with every beat of his heart.

"What have you done?" she asked.

His hand gripped her upper arm and began dragging her toward the throne. She fought against him, but Strahn held firm.

"Let go of me, you monster!"

He released her, throwing her back on the floor. "Monster?" he boomed. "You'll watch your tongue, or I'll cut it out."

"Do it then," she hissed.

He laughed, louder and crueler than anything she'd ever heard. "I claim you. From this day forth, you shall be mine, until such a time as I grow weary of that foul mouth of yours."

She sat up on the floor and spat, "I belong to no man."

"Not a man, human, but the High Ruler of Faerie. From the moment you came into my land, I became your master. And now I will take what is rightfully mine."

Twenty-Five

A silence settled on the room as the seconds ticked by, his words imprinting on the fae who sat wordlessly by. A minute passed, then a second, and still no one spoke. No one would. Ros was alone in this place, destined to be the plaything of the most powerful fae in the land.

There was a gasp from the crowd, breaking into the pervasive silence, but this time the crowd's surprise wasn't for Strahn. Ros followed their eyes to the entrance of the room. Telisa stood in the doorway, her face alight with a fury terrible to behold. Her hair blew in a breeze created from her own rage. She held a flaming sword in each hand, looking like death herself.

Beside her was Corbry, wounds healed, face glowing like a hero in the stories of old. Unlike his sister, who shone with a violent beauty, Corbry radiated an aura of wild desire that seemed to pour off him in savage waves. On all sides of him, fae had lost control; they showered themselves with drink, shoved food in their mouths by the fistful, lively in their overindulgent revelry.

On the outside of the siblings Ros knew were two others whom she didn't. They must be Penrose and Sarokia, the two siblings Luc had mentioned when she'd rescued him from the tomb. Ros could see by their appearances that they were related to Corbry, Telisa, and Sulien; just like the Spirits of the Air who had become her companions, these two were clearly powerful and fearsome to behold.

Whimsy forced their way into the room behind the siblings, so large that they tore a new entrance into the wall. A smear of sticky red matted their face. A roar escaped their massive, enraged form, showing teeth as long as Rosalinde's hand. She was terrified for anyone who got in their way.

Before any of them could cut through the crowd, Lucasian passed between them. He seemed to glide through the room rather than walk into it. He knelt over the bloody form of Sulien on the floor. When he placed his hands on Sulien's body, Luc's hands began to glow. Tendrils of golden flames paired with darkened shadows swirled around the injured fae.

Ros watched the cut on his neck stitch itself back together. The entire room seemed to hold its breath in anticipation. Seconds ticked by until finally, finally, Sulien's body shivered and he coughed. He climbed up on his hands and knees, gasped for breath, and pushed to his feet.

Luc rested a hand on Sulien's shoulder once he stood.

Power seemed to radiate through the restored fae at Lucasian's touch, until his gray-green eyes glowed like silver orbs. Sulien spoke, his voice echoing through the room with the force of a gale. "I said you will not have her."

Strahn left Ros where she was, stalking into the center of the room. "You're strong while you have a *Tuath Dé* at your back. But it doesn't matter. I've claimed her."

"You have no right," Luc said, his voice so quiet the whole crowd leaned forward to hear him.

"I take what I want," Strahn said through clenched teeth. "Didn't you learn that lesson the first time?"

"I learned you're a coward, a waste of breath. I learned you aren't worth the soil you sprouted from."

"Coming from the likes of you, I take that as a compliment."

"Let the girl go, Strahn."

"Or what? You're willing to wage a war and endanger all these people, *your* people, because I want to keep a human pet? That's not the Lucasian I know. He had his own share of pets, if I remember correctly. I do not think my memories have wavered while I've been free from your presence, though it has been a while."

"A thousand years, give or take."

"How did you get out of that tomb, anyway?"

Luc said, "It doesn't matter. I'm here now, and you won't get away with your vile machinations any longer."

Strahn stretched out his hands. A dark violet sphere appeared at his fingertips. "You know there will be casualties. Do you still want to do this?"

Lucasian's gaze skimmed the fae gathered around the chamber. When his eyes found Rosalinde's, she knew what he was going to do. She shook her head, begging him not to, but he only tilted his head higher..

"No, I will not endanger them."

"I'm glad you see reason." Strahn turned back toward Ros and smiled at her in a way that made her skin crawl.

"But you're not keeping the human, either."

Strahn spun on Luc, his fingers crackled with energy, as if he was desperate to release his anger on the newly freed *Tuath Dé*. "Then we are at an impasse."

"Take me instead."

"How about I take you in addition? Guards!"

Burly fae emerged from the shadows of the room. Ros wasn't sure how she'd missed them before. There were dozens of them moving to surround her friends. She reached for her power, felt the tingle of it in her bones, but it would not rise to meet her need.

With a cry like a wild animal, Whimsy charged. They blasted through four guards, throwing them to the side just as they had done to Corbry the day before. The Moonchild barreled down on her, but there was no time to move from their way. She crouched into a ball and hoped to avoid the worst of her collision.

But she didn't need to worry. As soon as Whimsy reached her, they swooped a massive paw down and scooped her up onto their shoulders even as they slid across the floor. They skidded to a stop at the apple core throne.

Whimsy swung one great fist toward the thing, blasting it to a pulp that flew into the crowd.

The decadent fae were distracted now, covered in the shredded flesh of the apple, but each of them was in danger even if they didn't see it. This was the best chance they had of escape. They needed a way out. The Unseelie Court had ushered the fae at the front of the room outside in between fighting the guards, but those in the middle and back of the room were trapped.

"Whimsy," Ros said into the Moonchild's ear, "can you clear a path out of here? Break down a wall if you have to, but we've gotta get the fae out of the room while we can."

She wasn't sure if they could control their rage in such a way. They couldn't remember their actions afterwards, so could they direct their anger while enraged?

In response, Whimsy threw themself against the wall, beating their massive fists on the stone. A few of the nearby fae had come out of the apple diversion and noticed what Whimsy was doing. Several with abilities came to help. With Whimsy's strength and the magic of the fae, they were able to create a path for the crowd to escape.

"We need to help Luc," Ros said as panicked fae streamed out into the night. Whimsy whirled back to the room. Telisa was wreaking havoc on anyone in the path of her flaming swords; Corbry and Sulien stood back to back, fighting a ring of brutes with horns on their heads as long as Rosalinde's arm. In the middle of it all, Lucasian and Strahn tangled. Their blows rained down on one another, neither seeming to have the advantage.

For the briefest second, Lucasian took his eyes away from Strahn and yelled, "Get her out of here!"

Whimsy bolted from the room, but Ros looked over her shoulder in time to see Strahn take that half second distraction as his opportunity. He struck Lucasian across the chest with a purple orb. Flames danced across the Night Lord's chest, wrapping his arms in magical chains, and he fell to the ground at Strahn's feet.

"No!" Ros yelled.

But it was too late. The fight was over. Lucasian had lost. As she and Whimsy bounded through the night, she realized, so had the rest of Faerie.

Twenty-Six

Once outside, Whimsy dropped to all fours and galloped through the fae lands. Ros clung to their fur with white-knuckled fists as she cried against them. She wanted to return for Lucasian, for the wind siblings, for anyone who would defy Strahn and needed her help.

But what help was a human girl against an enemy so powerful? The only thing she could do better than the others was find trouble. That's what had gotten her here in the first place.

And now here she was, running. Again. Being rescued. Again. Cassian had sent her away from the battle when he'd fought the darkness, he'd had Graeme fly her out of danger when she'd faced the distorted version of her mother at Earth house, and now, even in a completely different world, the only thing she could do was run from the danger the others so readily faced in her stead.

The only thing she'd done right since she got there was to make potent allies, and that was by sheer luck. Their allegiance was to Lucasian, not to her, despite how they'd come to her aid when she needed them most. The only other thing of value she'd been able to do was free the *Tuath Dé* from his tomb, but...

But nothing. That was the answer. She couldn't compete with the fae's power, and her magic was unreachable for whatever reason, but she'd been able to help Lucasian break the magic of his prison when no one else could. *That* was what she could do to save her companions.

"Whimsy," she called over the wind that rushed by them. An idea was taking hold in her mind. "We need to get back to my world now."

"Prince Luc wants you safe," they said, panting, "but I can't leave him. I must find a place to hide you before returning to his side."

"If you go back there, you'll die."

"Perhaps. It is a chance I will take for the Night Lord."

"Do you think there is a place in all of Faerie where I'll be safe from Strahn? And if you and the others are gone, surely I will be next. Is that what Luc would want?"

The Moonchild slowed their charge, their breath coming in hot, heavy gasps that frosted in the chill night air. After a moment, they said, "No, he would not want that."

"Good, because I have an idea to get us all out of this alive. I think I know how to save our friends. Do you trust me?"

"With my very life."

THEY STOOD at the edge of a dark forest, the trees stretching shadowed fingers over their heads. It was a place she had not yet seen in their travels, but something about it felt familiar all the same. There was power here, pulsing through the air, and Ros felt as if she could almost *feel* it calling out to her.

"Ready, young one?"

Ros nodded. She took one last look at the land around her, breathed in one last breath of Faerie air, and took her Moonchild's hand. They stepped through the veil and into the in-between world.

It wasn't the same as the first time she'd gone through. The sky was the color of Telisa's skin. The breeze carried the scent of clotted cream and strawberries, the same snack Corbry had eaten the night he'd been hurt. Streaks of silver and blue and brown shot across the sky, the same colors in Whimsy's fur. There was an aching music that seemed to hum in the space around them, whispering the tune of Lucasian's song.

Before she could detect all the sights and scents of this version of the in-between, Whimsy was pulling her through to the other side. Just like when she'd arrived in Faerie, the real world seemed to pale in comparison with the strange crossing point she'd just left. Melancholy pressed down on her, threatening to overpower her senses.

Unlike her first time through, Ros was certain that the difference this time was that she missed her new friends and worried for their safety. At least when she'd left this world, none of her family or friends were facing down a killer fae, just a jail sentence.

"How long were we in there?"

Whimsy shook their head. "I'm not positive. I can traverse the veil in minutes, but it's different when you travel with someone else. Two days, I think."

Ros nodded. "Today is the tenth day. My bargain with Lucasian is complete."

"I can take you to your father and lover," Whimsy said. "Prince Luc had me remove them to safety the first night we returned to the house, while you were still sleeping."

It made sense. Luc had promised to send his strongest warriors to rescue Cassian and her father. Who better than the Moonchild?

"Not yet. There's something I need to do first."

"Part of your rescue plan?"

Ros nodded, then asked, "Where is the closest Cradle?"

Whimsy pointed at their feet. Ros looked down at the darkened circle of earth. "I brought you through the veil near the place you would call the Air Cradle."

Ros laid on the ground, reaching out her senses to the magic flowing below her. She knew it was there; she had felt the power from the Faerie side of the veil. Still, she wasn't exactly sure what to expect, or *who* would be on the other side of that power. Ros felt something brush against her senses as the magic reached back, tentative and unsure.

Now that she knew what had happened, she imagined Lucasian had probably reacted the same way, though she hadn't noticed at the time.

The new force seemed to grow stronger, bigger, as it filtered through her mind. She showed it the memories of what had come before: absorbing the Night Cradle, going to Faerie, releasing Lucasian. She showed it the battle with Strahn and felt a surge of anger roiling through her as the fae brother she was tapped into tried to take over her mind. He wanted to rescue his brother, he wanted revenge, and he was ready to use her to get it.

No, she thought. *Only a small part of you can come with me. My mind isn't able to hold more. But once I have a sliver of your consciousness, we can free you fully from this tomb.*

A rush of magic filled her from toe to top until the very tips of her fingers felt as if they were floating. It was only for a second, or maybe less, and the feeling subsided. She let the magic settle for a moment inside her mind, and when she was certain she contained a portion of the brother, she asked, "Which one are you?"

Vidar, he growled, *Prince of the Dead.*

"Hang on, Vidar, and make room. We've got more brothers to find. You will all be free soon, to return to Faerie and take your rightful place."

"Vidar?" Whimsy asked.

Ros nodded. "A sliver of him, yes."

"And you can hold him as you did Luc?"

"All of them," Ros said. "I will raise an army of *Tuath Dé* to save Lucasian and the Spirits of the Air."

"Your promise is one of goodness, but are you certain you can do it? Your mortal body was not meant to possess the powers of the *Tuath Dé*."

"I can do it. Now tell me, which is closer: Fire, Water, or Earth?" Then, as if realizing there were only four brothers and five elements, including Luc's Night and Vidar's Air, she asked, "Who controls the fifth?"

"I believe you already know," Whimsy said. "Luc told me you saw the painting."

"Ombretta."

Whimsy nodded. "Here, she has fostered the gift of Night, but in Faerie, that was her brother's domain. She was the keeper of Fire, but the Fire tomb lies empty."

Ros scrubbed a hand over her tired eyes. She was still garbed in the uncomfortable dress Strahn had given her, though now it was dirty and ripped. She had no desire to pay a visit to the Night house ruler like this. Or in any condition, after learning she had abandoned Lucasian and the others. But it wasn't her grudge to hold.

"Water and Earth Cradles, then. We'll go to the Fire keeper last."

VISITING the other Cradles was much like the first. Whimsy gave her a location she recognized near each one, and fortunately, now that they were returned to her world, she could use shadow-walking to take them to each one. She knew now how to reach the fae brothers, even if she didn't fully comprehend how she was able to absorb them. The important thing was *that* she could, not how she could.

As she walked up the path to Ombretta's cottage, Ros had a mind full of fae and an ache in her chest. Carrying three fae was much more taxing than it had been with just Lucasian, and she was eager to finish her task and get them out of her.

The brothers didn't seem to mind being together, even just in small parts, and carried on a running conversation in her mind. One from which she couldn't seem to escape.

Telisa had been right about one thing, though— Mallory was the funny one. He'd been making jokes since she had retrieved him from the Water Cradle. First, they'd been self-deprecating, mainly about what he, as the Prince of Illusion, had been doing for the past millennium. Once they absorbed Faolan, Prince of Time, from the Earth Cradle, their youngest brother didn't hear the end of jokes about whether he'd gone through puberty yet or chosen to skip that part.

Ros knocked on the door. She wasn't sure what she'd do if Ombretta wasn't there. Did she even need her? Something in her gut said that she did, that they could only defeat Strahn if they were all together, but that could just be another human sentiment that didn't apply to the fae world. She wasn't sure how powerful Strahn was; he had overpowered her handily, but his strength against the other fae would be completely different. She hoped so, at least. When he had overthrown the *Tuath Dé* all those years before, he had been backed by others who were equally powerful when unified and able to join forces to force the brothers into their tombs. Even then they hadn't been strong enough to kill them. Perhaps Strahn's strength was only in his ability to convince others to join his cause, not having immense true power on his own as he wished everyone to believe.

Even as Ros thought it, she knew that wasn't true. Wishful thinking had kicked in with her desperation to save her friends, but that wasn't enough. She needed to get the *Tuath Dé* into action. Only one more thing to do, one more person to convince, and they could go after Lucasian.

The cottage door opened, and the dark-haired woman stood there wiping hands on an apron. She was lovely, far more beautiful than any mortal had a right to be, and Ros could fully see that now that she knew what to look for. There was a glow coming from her, a light that shone from her eyes, an otherness that marked her as *Tuath Dé*.

The voices in Rosalinde's head clamored at the sight of Ombretta, eager to see their long-lost sister. Their joy was palpable, and Ros felt buoyed by it despite the heaviness of their situation.

Ombretta smiled, but only for a second before a crease formed between her brows. "Rosalinde? Are you well? What has happened? Get inside!"

She grabbed Rosalinde's hand to pull her into the house. That's when she saw Whimsy. Ros felt Ombretta's grip tighten on her hand. Ombretta stepped in front of Rosalinde and called shadows to their fingers. In a quiet, firm tone, she asked, "Ros, did you make a bargain with this creature? Did you eat their food?"

That's no way to treat a Moonchild, little sister, one prince thought.

"I know them," Ros said. "They're not here to hurt me, or you, or anyone else."

"That has yet to be seen. The fae cannot be trusted," Ombretta said.

Ros put her hand on Ombretta's shoulder and said, "This fae can. I trust them with my life."

Ombretta released an exasperated sigh. "Go to my kitchen and find some bread. Now."

"I'm not under their control," Ros said.

It was clear her protests meant nothing. Ombretta would not believe Ros was free of the fae's hold, because her time in Faerie—and her time here—had made it clear that no one could be trusted.

Whimsy did something unexpected then—they bowed to Ombretta, giving dominion of themself away. "My name is Datura Whimsy. I have voluntarily served your eldest brother for many hundreds of years. You understand the significance of my actions at this moment?"

"Of course," Ombretta said. She swallowed, removed herself from between Whimsy and Ros, and said, "You'd better come in, too."

They moved their conversation to the sitting room where Ros had first been introduced to Cassian's mother. Back then, she was a mystery. She was the woman who nearly won her father's Great Match, who had secrets about the Night house, who kept things from her son about his older brother. Now, she was even more of an enigma. A fae who ran from her lands and hid among mortals, who never returned for her family, who hadn't even told her own children what they were.

Once they sat, Ombretta didn't mince words. "I feared my son was in danger, but now I see I should not have answered the door for you. Trouble has followed you to me instead."

"People often note that I am found most often with hardship at my side. I prefer to think that I am solving the problems no one else can. Even if I don't always recognize the answer right away."

"Why are you here?"

"Your brothers are in trouble."

Ombretta shook her head. "My brothers have been locked away longer than you've been alive. They aren't just in trouble—they're imprisoned under unbreakable magic. There is no hope for them."

"That may have been true before. Until I freed Lucasian."

Ombretta's eyes darted up. "How do you know his name?"

"The same way I know Vidar, Mallory, and Faolan. I freed Lucasian by accident, but the others I've released intentionally, so that they might return to Faerie and restore it."

"Faerie is lost to us," she said.

"It's easier to think that than to make an effort, I guess."

"That's not fair, Ros. You have no idea what it's been like for me."

"You mean running for your life, hiding away and letting us protect you, instead of fighting for your kingdom? I have a very good idea of what that is like, Ombretta. I've been doing the same thing these last few weeks. It feels terrible, and nothing else I do can fix the mistakes I've made to get myself in this situation. I'm sure you understand what I mean."

"You might think you understand what it's been like for me, the one who ran and hid, but I've been just as broken without them as I would have been locked in a tomb. I am just a wounded, lonely woman who has lost everyone she loved."

"Not everyone," Ros said, thinking of Cassian. But she nodded at the woman's words all the same, conceding that she didn't know the full extent of her stories, and probably never would. "Maybe it feels that way, and maybe it has been true through the years until this point, but there's a chance right now, and you may not get it again. Strahn has captured Lucasian, but he isn't expecting the rest of you to show up and take back your home."

"They were all turned against us, the Seelie and Unseelie Courts. There were too many to fight."

And we were caught unaware, Vidar thought.

"They've spent the last thousand years under Strahn's thumb. They've seen the error of their ways. They won't be against you this time. Your return to Faerie will be their restoration," Ros said.

"How would you know?"

"Because I just watched the Spirits of the Air—Sulien, Telisa, Corbry, Penrose, and Sarokia—fighting to protect Lucasian. I saw others who I can't name blowing holes in the wall of the High Ruler's ballroom to help their fellow fae escape Strahn. I don't know what became of them all, but before Whimsy and I escaped, they were battling on Lucasian's side."

Ombretta stood and paced the room. "If you're right..."

She is, Mallory thought.

"I am."

"...we may have a chance."

Ros held up a finger for a second, then said, "Vidar says it's time to bring the Fire."

Ombretta smiled, and Ros could finally see the resemblance between her and Luc. "It's time to do just that."

IN THE END, Ombretta, the brothers, and Whimsy all outvoted Ros when it came time to decide whether she could return to Faerie. Instead, Ombretta gave her three vials, and Ros placed a tear in each as she said goodbye to the brothers she may never meet outside of being voices in her head for a moment in time. Those strangers were the only hopes of saving her friends. Ros told Ombretta exactly how she'd entered Lucasian's tomb, trusting the results could be replicated by the *Tuath Dé*.

Ombretta put her hand on Rosalinde's shoulder. "I know you love my son. He loves you, too. He isn't always great at showing it, but if you choose to be with him, he'll spend every day trying to show you what you mean to him."

"I do love him," Ros said. "And I plan on telling him the first chance I get."

"Give him my love as well. I'll come back for him as soon as I can," Ombretta said. She took Rosalinde's hand and dropped a delicate ruby bracelet into it. "Wear this, as a sign of protection and friendship from Night house and the *Tuath Dé*. You have earned our favor, and our respect."

Ros fastened the bracelet on her wrist. She twisted her hand back and forth to watch the dark red stones. They seemed to catch even the smallest flicker of light and swallow it whole.

"Thank you."

Ombretta said, "No, dear, thank you. You've given my family back."

Ombretta stepped through the veil into the in-between.

As soon as Ombretta was gone, Ros felt the magical bond between her and Whimsy snap. She couldn't feel the pull of the Moonchild any longer, and though she never would have expected it ten days ago, Ros was devastated at the loss.

Whimsy put their hand on their chest and said, "Our path together is complete."

"How?" Ros asked.

"By returning the *Tuath Dé* to Faerie, you have done something no one else could do. You have taken my hand and walked with me on the last steps of the path I've walked for a thousand years. It took a human to save the fae."

"There's still so much to do," a sob coming out unexpectedly.

"And yet, your part is done. We'll fight on, as you will here, in your own kingdom. It is my dearest hope we meet again."

"Mine, as well."

Whimsy stood there, arms folded across their chest. As they looked down on Ros, the moon came out from behind a cloud, glowing down on the massive creature and turning them into the tiny thing she'd first met.

"I'm going to miss you," Whimsy said.

They reached up toward Ros, and she hugged them against herself. When they stepped back, Ros said, "You know, I think I like your other form. The hugs are way better."

Whimsy laughed, but a second later their face grew serious. "You've done something selfless this day. For though your time with Lucasian had passed, and you had already fulfilled your obligation to him, you continued to help."

She shrugged. "I had to. I can't leave Faerie with the

knowledge I've gained of that special place and not try to make it better."

"You're a strange human," Whimsy said, bowing. "I'm proud to call you my friend, Rosalinde Adara Managold."

Ros bowed to Whimsy, returning their power to them so that neither could control the other. "I'm at your service, Datura Whimsy, if ever you have need of me."

"And I yours," Whimsy said. "Call on me when you come into your kingdom. I should like to see the ruler you become."

"I don't know if that will happen. The road back won't be easy."

"If it were easy, you wouldn't take it. That is not your way."

"I suppose not."

"You may still doubt yourself, my young friend, but I do not. Your heart will find its home."

Whimsy stepped through the veil, leaving Ros alone in the forest on the spot of what would have been the Fire Cradle, if the tomb had not been empty, and the occupant on their way across worlds to start a revolution.

Twenty-Seven

Ros found Cassian and her father exactly where Whimsy had said she would. The old Night house was abandoned centuries before, leaving only ruins in its place, but there was enough shelter for the two men and they'd made themselves a comfortable area to rest against the southern wall.

When she stepped into what would have been a corridor in the house's former glory days, Ros saw them sitting together and smiled to herself, unable to help the joy that bloomed in her chest. They were both safe, both free, and she would make sure they stayed that way.

Cassian saw her first. He jumped from his seat and bounded to her, grabbing her by the waist and pulling her into his arms. She felt a thrill rush through her at being in his arms. He put her down, and they both laughed, overcome with delight at seeing one another.

After a moment, he asked, "What the devil are you wearing?"

"Oh, you know, just a dress given to me by a powerful fae who wanted to claim me for his own."

"Naturally," Cassian said. The look on his face was so relaxed at her words, it was as if he truly thought being kidnapped by the High Ruler of Faerie was the most normal excuse for her absence that she could give.

"Why are you still holed up in the old abandoned Night house? Why didn't you shadow-walk to somewhere more comfortable?"

"When a hulking fae creature rescues you from prison by barging through giant crystal walls and brings you to a seemingly safe place, telling you to stay put, you stay put."

"Naturally," she mimicked.

King Tancred was there now, standing in front of the reunited couple. Ros smiled at him, hoping to comfort him and ease his worry despite the situation, but there were tears pouring down his face.

"Rosalinde?" he asked.

"I'm sure you're scared after all you've been through, but I promise I'm going to make sure you are safe. I know you don't remember me, and that's fine, but I want you to know you can trust me. Do you at least remember me from the cell?"

"The cell?" His brows furrowed, and he said, "Darling, I remember you from your birth. I remember you from every sprained ankle, every splash of water from your untrained fingers, every time you called me 'Papa.' I remember every freckle on your nose and every hair on your head. You're my baby girl."

Rosalinde's jaw dropped at his words. *He remembers, he remembers.* She fell into his arms, overwhelmed by the relief and comfort of him knowing who she was. There was only one explanation: Whimsy had returned the memories. They didn't have to—their bargain was complete—but Ros knew they had done so because of their friendship, because of what they'd experienced together, and the bond they had formed outside of magic. She didn't know if they'd returned them to everyone or just him, but right now, it didn't matter. She had her father back, she had Cassian at her side, and she was home.

Home, in her kingdom, the place she loved and served. Ros had been returned to the people she would fight for, no matter the cost. As much as she worried for her fae friends and the kingdom of Faerie, her battle was here. She had done everything she could to rescue Lucasian and free those lands from Strahn, but now their destiny was in their own hands, and hers was here in Talabrih.

Rosalinde looked out over the ruins of the Night house castle and the trees beyond. This place was full of so much history that she didn't understand, but more than that, it held a future that had yet to be written. She would not let things continue as they had for the last thousand years, guided by those who operated only for power and greed. No, Ros had her hand on the pen, ready to write the next chapter for Talabrih; it would be one of prosperity, equity, and justice for all people, not just those who could afford to buy a better future.

This land was broken, but it was her home. No matter what came next for her, she would fight for it, broken pieces and all.

With renewed resolve, Rosalinde said, "We can't waste any more time. So much has already been lost because I didn't know, because I didn't understand. But I get it now. Talabrih needs us more than ever."

Cassian nodded, his eyes full of unwavering support. "I'm with you, Ros. Wherever you lead, I will follow. Always."

King Tancred stared at Ros, his periwinkle gaze showing an intensity she'd never seen before. "I may not have my full strength back yet, but I will fight by your side, my daughter."

"You're a Healer. Every day of your life has been inclined toward fixing the broken. Will you be able to fight, knowing what will happen to those who oppose us?" Ros asked.

"It won't be easy," Tancred said.

Ros put her hand on her father's shoulder and said, "No one will think less of you for sitting this out. It goes against your very nature."

"My life is to serve Talabrih. I will do that however I am needed."

Ros held out her hands toward them. "Let's go then."

"Where first?" Cassian asked.

Ros took a deep breath, exhaled, and said, "Air House."

Twenty-Eight

They walked through the shadows. Though Ros could use the Night abilities now, she let Cassian take the lead. Her control over the foreign abilities was tentative, and she wanted to practice using them when their lives weren't at stake. Besides, Ros wasn't exactly sure how they would get into Air house with the magic poisoning preventing the use of magic in the place.

Cassian knew. Without knowing what Ros would do when she returned for them, he had planned and prepared for any eventuality. He dropped them out of the shadows and onto the spire Ros had jumped off only days before.

Ros felt a sense of foreboding as soon as their feet touched solid ground. When she was younger, Ros and Larkin had made up stories about Air house, painting it as a place of darkness and mystery. They hadn't believed any of the things they'd said, but had wanted to entertain one another with wild and unbelievable tales, as friends often do. Now, Ros knew the horror stories were more true than they had imagined.

The night was clear and cold; stars twinkled above, sparkling against the sea-lavender spires. Cassian was on alert, eyes scanning the area for any sign of guards. Rosalinde trusted him enough to let her own gaze wander. She stared out at the imposing structures, her mind flitting between ideas as she tried to figure out her first move.

Ros felt a strange throbbing at her wrist and looked down at the bracelet Ombretta had given her. Color and light seemed to swirl into the stones, and with each second that ticked by Ros felt heat radiating out from her wrist. Despite how hot it seemed to get, the bracelet did not burn her. Whimsy's words came back to her then, reminding Ros of who had given her the charm: *Ombretta was the keeper of Fire.*

Reaching for the powers she hadn't felt since she first came to Air house, Ros was surprised to find a spark burning in her gut. Though she couldn't feel the other elements, Ombretta's bracelet at least afforded her a little protection from the magic poisoning.

She turned to Cassian and King Tancred, saying, "Stay close, be ready for anything."

They made it to the prison spire without a single guard spotting them. Rather than buoy Rosalinde's spirits, it made her nervous. Someone should be keeping guard, and if they weren't, there was a problem. The trio climbed the ladder into the spire and ascended the steps. When they reached her father's former cell, a laugh bubbled up from

Rosalinde's gut. A Whimsy-sized hole was torn out of the side of the spire.

"Why did Whimsy tear a hole into the side of the room to get you out of here?" she asked.

"I wasn't brave enough to ask," Cassian said.

Tancred smiled. "I think it was more about them getting in than us getting out. The entrances are too small for a creature of that size."

"Whimsy can travel in a similar manner to Cassian. They should have been able to pop into the room, grab you, and leave in seconds."

Cassian shrugged. "A mystery to solve the next time you see them."

The thought sent a nervous shudder through Ros. She dearly hoped to see her fae friends again, but had no idea when or if that would happen. As much as she wanted to think on how to make it happen, she couldn't afford to dwell on it right now. She had sent all the help she could, and now she needed to focus on solving her own troubles.

They continued up to Cordelia le Fevre's cell. The atmosphere in the spire was oppressive, a constant reminder of the suffering that had taken place within these walls. Though Cordelia and her father were physically taken care of while imprisoned, the emotional turmoil they'd experienced was soul crushing.

Ros looked through the floor to ceiling window into the room beyond but couldn't see the Fire house noble. There was nowhere to hide in the room, nowhere to escape for the smallest amount of privacy. Even her toilet was visible from Rosalinde's vantage point. Tentatively Ros asked, "Cordelia?"

Cassian put his hand on Rosalinde's shoulder and said, "She's not here."

"What has happened to her?"

"Maybe they moved her after we escaped," Tancred said.

"I don't know," Cassian said, "but we can't stick around to find out. There are others who need us."

Ros put her hand against the empty chamber window, her eyes scanning one last time. She hated to think of what might have befallen the girl in the days she had been in Faerie. Every scenario her mind went to was worse than the next. With Graeme Monsanato's charming facade hiding the truth of who he was and what he was capable of, Ros wasn't sure what to expect from the Air house mage.

They went back down through the tower, passing empty rooms on each floor. Ros was glad the rooms hadn't been filled with new prisoners, but the missing noble-woman from upstairs had her worried. Without her, Ros would instead need to start the next part of her plan. It was much more uncertain, and Ros couldn't be sure it would work.

She led Cassian and her father across the icy bridge she had crossed with Henry when she was pretending to be a maid. Ros had been afraid the first time, but now she knew the bridges were spelled for safety. She couldn't fall, even if each step made her feel like she would.

They went into the large spire, and it took a moment

for Ros to get her bearings. She had been so lost that day after learning that the memory of her existence had been removed from the minds of all who knew her, and so absolutely terrified from her experience with Graeme that Ros hadn't paid any attention to where Henry was taking her. It had been fortunate that such a kind soul had been the one to find her. Now, she hoped to find him.

They ventured lower through the spire, the structure turning in on itself as they descended the curving path carved through the building. The corridors were empty, but rather than fortunate, Rosalinde's skin prickled with unease. Finally they reached a plain wooden door that opened to reveal a row of small rooms, barely large enough to hold the small bed and table. Each had a curtain either pushed to the side or drawn closed in front of the room's archway.

"Where are the prisoners?" Ros whispered.

"These aren't cells, darling," King Tancred said. "These are the servants' quarters."

The air was heavy with a palpable sense of despair. The rooms might not be cells, but they were certainly full of prisoners. Each face that peeked around the curtain held a captive with questioning eyes, their faces etched with years of torment. Ros met the gaze and gave a nod toward the young woman who had told her about staying dirty to reduce trouble for herself. The girl wordlessly closed the curtain to her room.

"King Tancred," a man said.

Ros turned to see Henry giving a slight bow to her father.

"Hello, Henry," Tancred said.

"Why have you returned?"

Tancred put his hand on the man's slumped shoulder and said, "To help."

Henry's eyes shone with hope for the briefest second before his face clouded over again. "You shouldn't be here. Your presence will bring nothing but trouble for us."

Ros watched as more curtains closed. Things were not going the way she wanted. Up ahead, she saw a blonde head lean past the curtain of her room. She stared at Ros from hollow eyes with black circles underneath. Despite the change in her appearance over the last few days, it was most certainly the noble daughter of Fire house. Rosalinde approached Cordelia le Fevre, her heart aching at the sight.

"We've come to set you free," she said.

"You can't fight them," Codelia said. "You can't fight this *place*."

Cassian said, "Not alone. Together we might have a chance."

"Together?" a voice asked from behind a curtain. "Since when does the crown care for the likes of us."

"We're here because there's no other option," another voice said.

"There are options," Ros said. "We'll find work for you, we'll build homes. You are no longer prisoners of Air House. It's time to rebuild your lives."

"There's nothing left of our lives," Cordelia said.

Ros turned to see Henry bowing his head. "I wish things were different, my King, I truly do."

Rosalinde swallowed back her pain and frustration. She hadn't expected things to be easy for them, but she also hadn't expected their mission to be so bleak. The malevolent grip of Air House held firm, unwavering against their good intentions. They would need to find help if they were going to make any headway. Standing and falling against Air house was one thing, but the true battle for Talabrih's future lay ahead. They could not risk failing again.

Rosalinde turned to her father and spoke with conviction, "Today is not the day we hoped for, but together we will bring about the change Talabrih desperately needs. We will unite our kingdom, empower our people, and ensure justice and equity for all."

With the weight of her destiny upon her shoulders and her loved ones at her side, Rosalinde knew she was ready to move on to the next page for Talabrih. The new installment would be one of hope, courage, and a brighter tomorrow.

"We'll win no one today," Tancred said. "Let's get out of here while we still can."

Heartbroken, Ros asked, "Will none of you come with us? Will none of you try?"

"I'll go," Cordelia said. "Even if Graeme throws me from this prison himself, I'd rather have a quick death than spend another second under his thumb."

Ros reached out to touch the woman's shoulder, but Cordelia flinched away. Whatever Graeme had done to her was bone deep, and it would take a long time to heal those wounds.

They left the servants' chambers behind and climbed through the spire. As soon as they stepped out into the cold night air, a sudden gust of wind swirled around them, carrying a sinister presence. Emerging from the shadows, Graeme materialized before them. His eyes glinted with malevolence, and a wicked smile twisted his lips.

"Ah, Rosalinde," Graeme sneered, his voice dripping with malice. "I see you've returned to me, and you've brought gifts. Couldn't stay away?"

Rosalinde clenched her fists at her side as fire burned through her veins. She glanced at Cassian, whose eyes locked onto hers, a silent affirmation of their shared determination.

Graeme raised his hand, and a cyclone of razor-sharp wind blades whirled into existence around him. The maelstrom threatened to tear them apart. With a wave of his hand, he sent the deadly projectiles hurtling toward Rosalinde and her group.

Rosalinde's instincts kicked in. Though she could only claim the use of fire while subject to the magic poisoning the space around them, it was enough. She summoned a wall of flame to shield them from the onslaught, the blades of wind crashing harmlessly against her protective barrier and fizzling to nothing.

As the smoke cleared, Graeme's laughter filled the air. "Impressive, Rosalinde, especially considering you are a Water mage. Tell me, where did you learn those tricks?"

"There's more where that came from," she yelled back.

"I hope so. It's always more fun fighting someone who doesn't immediately cower. But make no mistake, you will bow before me."

With a flick of his fingers, he created a vacuum, sucking the air out of the immediate surroundings. Rosalinde and her companions gasped for breath, their chests tightening in the absence of air.

Rosalinde clawed at her throat as if she could open it up to breathe again. Reaching toward Graeme with her other hand, she sent a spear of fire hurtling toward his chest. He jumped out of the way at the last second, releasing his hold on the air around them. Amidst the chaos, Rosalinde and her people pushed forward. They could do little in this place, but if they could make it to the uppermost tower where the effects didn't reach, there would be a chance for them to survive.

Ros couldn't see where Graeme had ducked off to, but she sent a barrage of fireballs careening through the night in the direction he had gone.

"Run," she said to the others. "We must get to the tower."

Cordelia was in no condition to sprint—her body and mind were weak from her imprisonment in Air house. Without the use of his powers, Tancred couldn't heal her. Fortunately, Cassian was able to swoop into action. He bowed his head and cautiously reached a hand forward.

"Let me help."

After a second, Codelia gave a terse nod and Cassian

picked up the girl, racing across the bridges and through the night.

"You need to go too," Ros said to her father.

"I won't leave without you."

"That's right, you won't. I'm not staying here for heroics, or to fight a battle I can't win."

Realization had finally hit Ros. Yes, she ran, and yes, it often felt like giving up; still, she couldn't win the war if she was dead. Sometimes running was the only option, whether she liked it or not.

Again she scanned the area for Graeme, but the Air Elementalist was nowhere to be seen. Ros backed across the bridge after her father, afraid to turn her back on the last place she'd seen Graeme. Her father directed her to the tower they'd entered through shadow-walking, and as soon as she reached the top Ros could feel the pressure of the magic poisoning release a bit.

Graeme's voice rang out from somewhere below them where he remained hidden in the shadows. "This isn't over. You can run, you can hide, but sooner or later your time will come."

Ros wanted to yell something back, some clever quip to instill fear in Graeme for what was to come. She wanted to challenge him and force him out of hiding to face her in a fair fight, not one where most of her access to elemental magic was constricted and what she did have was new to her. Rosalinde wanted to make Graeme give up his hold on the people of Air house, to watch as they abandoned him for the hope of a better future, a better Talabrih.

But she didn't. She couldn't. No matter what she wanted, Rosalinde's options were few: get captured, or run away. There was no thinking her way out of this situation, or even fighting her way out. This was a battle she could not win.

Cassian put his hand on her shoulder and said, "Let's go, love. There's nothing more to do."

He was right, she knew, but the thought of leaving chafed her. "It doesn't feel right abandoning all those people. Especially now that I know the truth about Graeme."

"I know," he said, "but leaving today means you'll have a chance to fight for them again."

"And all the other people in the kingdom who need you," her father said.

Codelia's voice, faint in the wind buffeting them, said, "This isn't the end."

Ros nodded as she swallowed back the lump forming in her throat. "No, it isn't. Our fight is just beginning."

Afterword

Thank you for reading *A Memory of Air House.* I hope you enjoyed the continuation of Rosalinde's adventure! If you did, please leave me a review, stop by my website, or find me on social media. I'd love to hear from you. You all mean the world to me and I'm truly thankful for the time you've given my book.

If you'd like to try another story with royals, magic, and new book boyfriends, check out my mermaid series starting with *Black Sea Bright Song.*

You may also like my sci-fi series under Shelly Jarvis: The Book of the Golden One duology starts with *The Dreamwalker* or the 3-book post apocalyptic series Little Star begins with City of Trials.

About the Author

Michelle Jarvis is a fantasy romance author with a penchant for royalty. She loves diverse characters and believes everyone deserves a love story.

While Michelle has had her own love affair with writing since she was in elementary school, it wasn't until her thirties that she realized how much fun it was to turn up those romantic subplots. Now she's combining her love of fantasy and her newfound passion for romance to put them into the hands of readers.

Michelle lives in West Virginia with her partner and their rescue dogs–Gimli, Gus-Gus/Gooser/Goosie-boy, Pickles, and Fergus.

For free books, bonus scenes, and news about upcoming releases, sign up for Michelle's mailing list on her website: www.authormichelle.com

Also by Michelle Jarvis

City of Trials

"Lady *Mad Max* meets LGBTQ+ *Hunger Games*"

The Dreamwalker

"*Space Harry Potter*"

Black Sea Bright Song

"*The Little Mermaid* if it was told from Ursula's point of view"

Writing for Weirdos: How to Craft Compelling Short Fiction